Sid retired in 2010 after thirty-five years of primary school teaching (over twenty-five as a Head). During those decades many amusing things were said or done by children and adults, or strange scenarios occurred at his four schools.

On such occasions people often say, "I must remember that!" He has tried to keep a record of as many of these as possible and this has been the basis for the content. All the stories and events have actually happened (mainly to him), though all names and often genders have been changed.

The wonderful illustrations have been created by Kerry Bryant, an ex-pupil from his final primary school. She hopes to have a successful career in the world of creative media in the not too distant future.

MISS ING – LINK TEACHER (RQT)

Recently Qualified Teacher

By the same author:

Miss Ing – Teacher (NQT)
Pegasus (2012)

ISBN: 978 1 903490 77 8

Sid Wales

MISS ING – LINK TEACHER (RQT)

Recently Qualified Teacher

Very Best Wishes,

Sid Wales

Pegasus

PEGASUS PAPERBACK

A CIP catalogue record for this title is
available from the British Library

ISBN-978 1 903490 83 9

*Pegasus is an imprint of
Pegasus Elliot MacKenzie Publishers Ltd.*
www.pegasuspublishers.com

First Published in 2013

**Pegasus
Sheraton House Castle Park
Cambridge CB3 0AX England**

Printed & Bound in Great Britain

Dedication

To my two sons Ian and Adam

Acknowledgements

Thank you to everyone at:

a) St Mary's C of E, Thornbury

b) Loxwood Primary School

c) Ramsey St Mary's Primary School

d) The Rackham C of E , Witchford, Ely

Many thanks to Lesley Gallois for all her support and encouragement with this book.

Contents

CHAPTER ONE

HERE WE GO AGAIN – SECOND TIME LUCKY?

My first year of teaching was a hard one, very enjoyable (most of the time) but tough, or as the modern phrase goes 'a steep learning curve'. I now have it confirmed in writing by someone from the Department of Education, or whatever its name is this year, that I am a fully qualified teacher. I have successfully completed my first year as a member of the teaching profession so I am no longer a member of the 'NQT Club' (Newly Qualified Teacher).

However, the following week I received a letter from my local authority informing me that I had risen to the dizzy heights of RQT (Recently Qualified Teacher). Apparently this is a fairly new set of letters to burden new recruits to teaching, a bit like displaying those green and white 'P plates' on your car even after you really have just passed your driving test. Maybe next year when I will be a Third Year Qualified Teacher, TYQT would be a cool set of initials, especially if pronounced 'ticked' – very appropriate for a teacher! Or if that was too long I could just be a Third Year Teacher, a TYT. Then I could be a FYT the academic year after that.

My second year at St Alemate's CE looked like having a beefy start. What with Miss (or Ms) Steak as the new Headteacher this year, Mrs Bull as my new Teaching Assistant and a new boy called Steven Cowell. I wonder what delights my new group of children had in store for me, no Seans on my class list but a few other suspicious looking names especially an Elvis, Bradley, Tyler, Marcus and Charley (male and female).

I thought back to my first few days at school last year with the vision of me causing a traffic jam in the staff car park without realising it, Sean up the tree, everyone's class lined up straight on the first morning and mine scattered far and wide, slipping through the faulty chair in the staffroom, the list goes on.

First morning of a new school year was always a special one tinged with excitement even for the experienced, gnarled cynics of the staffroom. A new Headteacher in addition to that made everyone slightly on edge. My experienced teacher colleagues have told me that there were two types of 'newbie' Head. First, there were the trendy ones who were keen to make their mark early, came in like a whirlwind and changed everything – even decreased the number of doors on classrooms and chairs in the classrooms throughout the school. Second were the cunning ones who changed absolutely nothing initially, came in and took stock of everything and everyone. Then after about six months when all the staff had relaxed, the merry-go-round of fun could begin.

All the teaching staff had arrived before the scheduled meeting start time even the new NQT, Miss Cheeseburger – I think her relatives were German. Unlike me last year, she had arrived early, but exactly like me a year ago she sat in THE chair. As usual for such occasions both the male teachers in the school, Mr Bubble and Mr Hart, went and sat down directly opposite her and waited for the entertainment to commence. Right on time Miss Steak arrived and welcomed everyone especially her fellow first-dayer, Maria.

Miss Steak set out her stall by announcing how pleased she was to be the new Headteacher and how hard and busy a year it was going to be for everyone. I noticed a few eye contact glances being made between the senior citizens of the staff group at that particular sentence. There was a little squeak at that point as the first stage of Miss Cheeseburger's journey downwards started through the chair of the ever expanding springs. Miss Steak glanced across at her but no one else bothered at this early stage of the chair-initiation. As Miss Jos Steak continued talking about her review of all school policies and everyone's role in their process, Maria Cheeseburger continued on her journey south, down through the smiling mouth of the chair trap door. By now her bottom was midway between the floor and where it had started when she first sat down. The two men were looking happier by the minute, the women teachers oozed sympathy for their new NQT colleague. "Are you all right Maria?" enquired Miss Steak.

"Yes, fine thank you," she replied trying to hoist herself a little higher by pushing down on the arms of the chair. But it was too late and the chair (sometimes called 'Jaws') had a very firm hold of her with no intention of an early release. Our Headteacher started on her last point before the end of the meeting, her final and most important one before we left to collect our classes. Unfortunately, at the crucial point of delivery, Maria shot through the chair. Her bottom rested on the floor, white knickers for all to see with the two men making sure they had a full view of the Winnie the Pooh pictures that were printed on the underwear. Poor Maria created a symbolic 'V' shape but by the time she had been rescued from the clutches of Jaws, the tears of embarrassment were flowing down her face. I felt a little guilty that maybe I should have said something to her, but I had to overcome my own problems this morning and any thoughts of that were far from my head.

We hurried away to complete the last minute sorting out before our new classes walked through the door full of their new school year anticipation and enthusiasm. Little did we know that by the time we returned to the staffroom for our first mid-morning break of the school year Miss Steak would have made her first executive decision. One chair would be missing from the staffroom and Jaws expelled. It was a permanent exclusion from the room where it had claimed countless victims – much to the obvious disappointment of two certain male teachers.

The children were full of stories about what they had been up to during the long break, but teachers have to be very careful because there will always be children in the class, through no fault of their own, who haven't been away at all. My own summer holidays had gone well and I had taken the opportunity to visit Helen, my best friend from when I was at University, who lived in New Zealand. Travelling was something I had routinely avoided, a short journey in Boris being bad enough, but to travel to the other side of the world had seemed out of the question. But the chance of a cheap flight deal came up and I grabbed it. Two weeks in Kiwi-land was really not enough, there was so much to see and do there. Jumping off a cliff attached to a thin piece of elasticated rope is probably not everyone's idea of fun but the visit to three vineyards had helped me pluck up the courage to give it a go. One hundred metres high up a mountain side with a dribble of water down below looked a non-starter to me as my legs turned to jelly and I felt very faint. But the push in the middle of my back gave me all the encouragement I needed to swallow dive kicking and screaming all the way down and trying really, really hard not to wet myself from fear.

Just at the point when I thought my time had come and death was close, the rope pulled me back and I catapulted back up again but thankfully only a quarter of the distance. By the time I had finished bouncing around like a kangaroo in the mating season I had convinced myself, and anyone who asked, that it was the greatest thing I had ever experienced. Helen was an old hand at these frightening things and just took it in her stride.

It was a good thing I liked rugby, it seemed like they did nothing else out there but play rugby, analyse the last game played or talk about the one coming up next, they actually have one TV channel devoted to it twenty-four hours a day!

The helicopter ride around the mountains of the Southern Alps was breath-taking, and to see the area that was used for a lot of the filming on the Lord of the Rings and Hobbit series was sensational. Jet boat riding was simply exhilarating with the 360 degree turns just stomach churning and great fun. There was so much to see and do in New Zealand but there wasn't enough time to do it all. As one of the locals said to me,

"New Zealand is a much better place than the Old Zealand."

I have never come across such a friendly nation of people and the history of the Maori culture was incredible. The whole experience was exhausting especially with about 23 hours of flying time to reach it and a 12 hour time difference to adapt to. My body clock rapidly needed a rewind, good job I had a week left of my summer holidays before the start of the new term.

CHAPTER TWO

CZECH MATE

After Mr Bush's rather sudden departure there was no one willing, or able, to carry on our very successful Chess club. The school asked for a volunteer via the newsletters sent out by the village as well as St Alemate's. Miss Steak also mentioned it several times at our staff meetings if anyone was willing to take it on, whether they could play chess or not. That seemed a bit odd to me, why would you take on a club like that if you didn't know the rules?

At my next playground duty I was approached by several of the older children about running the Chess club. My first reaction was to laugh but they didn't join in, they were very serious. Some of the group had been in my class last year, others I only knew by sight, as for the rest, I didn't even know their names. After attempting to explain to them that I had never played, they quickly responded by telling me that they could teach me the rules and how to organise everything just like Mr Bush had run it. We left it that I would think about it and I'd let them know next week.

It came as a bit of a shock when I was thanked by my Headteacher at the end of the following Monday's staff meeting for agreeing to take over the school Chess club. Despite my early mutterings of disagreement there were smiles all around the room, accompanied by 'well dones' and a round of applause. I think I had been well and truly set up by the Year 5/6 chess mafia. After school the next day I went to our local library to find a few books that might help me fill my void of chess knowledge. I was amazed how many books there were from ones with more pictures than words to very complicated ones by grand masters and world champions. There was even one called 'How to Cheat at Chess', this rather shattered my overall impression and image of the quiet board game.

At the end of the week, I put up a small notice to give the children a chance to sign up for the Chess Club if they were interested in joining. I deliberately did not ask for it to be mentioned in Assembly or written on a newsletter. You can imagine my shock to discover forty names from Key Stage 2 children just three days later. They were so keen that someone had added another sheet of blank paper as I hadn't left enough space on my small notice. What a headache, I was already doing my regular after school Recorder Club. There were too many children to take them all at once and we didn't have twenty chess sets anyway. So I decided to run it on a Thursday, half at lunchtime and the other half after school. That was also my afternoon out of the classroom for planning, preparation and assessment time so it would work out well, I hoped.

Over that weekend I read my books and used a computer program that one of the staff had given me to practice some moves. It was a really complicated game at first but when you remembered all the names of the pieces, how they moved and took, it started to mean something. In the first few weeks, things gradually began to take shape. I was fine with the younger ones at lunchtime. I even managed to win a few games when there was an odd number of children. On such occasions I was needed to step in and make up the numbers. But most of the older ones were beyond me and they ended up telling me more and more about the game, strategies and tactics.

The following Friday afternoon there was a note left on my desk from the school secretary, Mrs Ored, telling me to expect a new pupil on Monday morning. Apparently, he was from the Czech Republic and the family had only just arrived in England, his name was Vladi Noosenz.

After a fairly quiet weekend, Monday morning seemed to come around very quickly. About ten minutes before the start of school, Miss Steak turned up with Vladi and his parents. The mother spoke no English and the father only a few words; Vladi took after his mother linguistically. How was I expected to teach a nine year old in a class of thirty children when he had no knowledge of English? Miss Steak said that the school was applying for emergency funding to employ a part-time Teaching Assistant to work with him for some of the week, but that might take a while to happen. I sent Mrs Bull off to the Foundation stage classrooms to try and find a few books that might help him to start with and I took Vladi down to the playground to meet a few specially selected members of my

Chess Challenge

class who would show him around and look after him. They found communication very difficult but a few improved their dramatic, facial expression and body language skills. I felt really sorry for Vladi and Mrs Bull, all her time now had to be spent with him rather than the group of children she usually worked with. He didn't go into Assembly with the rest of the class, what was the point? I kept him back with me to try and learn a few key words. Twenty minutes later, a few of his new found friends returned to collect him after the whole school Assembly.

Talking to other staff over break time about my new problem child made the short time go doubly quick. There were a few sensible suggestions but nothing that could go very far to helping without the aid of an extra person. As we walked down to the Key Stage 2 playground after the mid-morning break it was obvious before the children were in view that something was wrong. The whistle was blowing but the noise was still very loud from the children. As we approached, the noise turned into chanting but it was difficult to tell exactly what they were saying. It sounded like the names of two children, but being shouted at the same time distorted both words. The two male teachers looked at each other and chorused the same word in unison, "fight".

I was told that there were very few fights at our school but when they happened it could be nasty. Our two male teachers left us behind at this point with Phil Hart doing a sprint jog and Barry Bubble rolling from side to side doing the best he could to move quicker than walking pace. As the playground came into view the sight was very worrying, nearly all the older children were in one corner of the tarmac forming a large circle with half on one side chanting one name and the other half singing a different name. I could just make out the two different words and a chill went through my body. The two names being shouted by the hordes were Sean and Vladi. Surely my new child, with no spoken English, was not in a fight with an older boy on his very first break time? Mrs Quaver was making a tuneful noise on her whistle and trying to find her way through the crowd but without success. Mr Hart reached the throng and dived straight in, partly disappearing from sight, while Mr Bubble had so far only made it halfway across the playground.

When Mr Hart made it through the children into the centre point of the commotion he was stunned to find the new Year 4 boy and tree climber Sean heavily involved head to head…in a game of Chess! Apparently Vladi had been walking around with his new, young interpreters when they came across the large chess pieces in the corner. Vladi's face had lit up with excitement so they set them up for a game when Sean Hitts, the best chess player in the school, turned up and challenged him to a game. Vladi recognised the body language of being offered a match, shook hands with his opponent and the game had begun. No one usually bothered to play Sean at chess, for one he was odd and for another he was very good. After about ten minutes into the game, word started to spread that Sean was losing to the new foreign boy a year younger. Five minutes later almost all the older children were trying to catch a glimpse of this unusual spectacle. The last person to beat Sean from St Alemate's was Mr Bush, (the previous Headteacher) nearly two years ago. All the Year 5 and 6 children were standing around Sean's half of the board on three sides cheering on their champion, and all the younger ones were solidly behind their new hero Vladi, whoever he was. Both camps chanted the name of the child in their half of the age group at the same time, attempting to drown out the other half. Chess has its own international language. You don't need to speak a word. The rules are the same all over the world.

Vladi was definitely ahead on pieces in the position on the board. He looked confident and was showing the body language of someone with a final plan to win the board battle. Unfortunately, it was just at this moment when the clumsy Mr P Hart arrived on the scene, to be more accurate he arrived on the board that was painted onto the tarmac and scattered most of the remaining pieces that were still a part of the game north, south, east and west. There was a disappointed gasp of dismay from the Year 3 and 4 children and a cheer of relief from the smiling older spectators.

"We'd best call it a draw then Vladi," said a grinning Sean and offered his right hand towards his worthy opponent, "See you at Chess Club on Thursday."

He then turned to Mr Hart with a look of gratitude and said,

"Nice one Mr Hart, sir, I owe you." At that all the children started to drift away towards their class lining up marks only to be met by Mr Bubble just arriving on the scene looking very hot, red, bothered and out of breath.

In a matter of around fifteen minutes, Vladi had become the most popular child in the class. He could now speak about ten words of the English language, although I told him that I never wanted to hear him say two of them ever again. The children did everything they could to help him inside and out of the classroom. His cult status was further confirmed when they discovered he was also good at football.

CHAPTER THREE

THE SADDEST DAY OF MY LIFE

The following week started similar to many Monday mornings. My alarm clock went off and I thought it must be a mistake. Surely I had not been in bed very long? Close scrutiny of those digital numbers at my side confirmed that indeed it was my usual wake up time. Why does it feel more unreal on Mondays rather than on any other week day?

My first working morning of the week went from bad to worse. In an effort to give my teeth a thorough clean I brushed out part of a filling on a back molar. My usual daily hot shower felt like the water had been piped directly from the Arctic. Apparently, there had been a power cut during the night and it had turned off the water heater switch. With ease I managed to put my big toe through the end of my only school worthy pair of tights. I could only hope that they survived the day and didn't ladder all the way up my leg.

Time was getting on now and at breakfast, in my rush, I overloaded the cereal spoon and a solid lump fell overboard and splashed belly flop style into the deepest part of the milk, causing a mini tidal wave to crash over the edge of the bowl and run down the front of my blouse. My mother was hovering. She hadn't said a word yet, she just hovered. If she ever went on that Mastermind quiz programme her specialist subject would be 'hovering'.

"Sarah darling…" she started.

"No Mum. Thanks Mum, no time Mum. Bye Mum," and I made my exit from the breakfast table as quickly as a sprinter out of the blocks at the start of the 100 metre Olympic final. With a bit of luck, I would be through the door before she had finished her opening sentence of the day, or at worst be far enough away to truthfully admit that I hadn't heard her motherly words of wisdom.

On the final leg of my mad dash to the car through the hallway, I leant over slightly to the right to pick up my school briefcase and to the left for my coat off the peg and I was free… or perhaps not. "Morning Boris," I said cheerfully to my faithful friend and car (even if he was a 2CV). "How are you this Monday morning my dear, fine, unwashed friend? What's that? You can't see? Oh, of course the drop in temperature has misted up the windows. That's not a problem old chap, back in a minute."

I quickly found a cloth and went around the windows to wipe away the condensation and sat back behind the wheel again, "How's that then Boris? What do you mean who turned the daylight off?" Wow, yes it was much darker outside than 5 minutes ago. Was it an eclipse that I had forgotten about, was it the end of the world? Had someone turned off the sun? No I had just used a cloth that was covered in oil after mopping up Boris at the weekend when he had a leak. The oil slick had

Devalued Boris

now spread all around the car creating a makeshift black-out on all his windows. Aaaahgh! I thought noisily inside my head. What else could possibly go wrong on this Monday morning! I turned the ignition key to hear ... nothing.

I turned it to the off position to try again but with the same result. "No Boris, don't do this to me please," I uttered out loud. Third time lucky they say, but who says?? Who was the first idiot, sorry, person to mutter those stupid three words? I closed my eyes, turned the ignition to OFF and then to ON! Nothing. No, not quite nothing there was a noise, a little tapping noise in groups of three. Was it the engine? Was it our local woodpecker? Was it Morse code? Was it my Mother?

What! No it can't be, no, anything but my Mother, please, no, no, not this early on a Monday morning school day!

Yes it was Mum. "Hello Mum," I said after slowly rolling down my window (no electric windows in a 2CV).

"Charge," said my Mum. "Charge!" she said even louder.

I was trying to compose myself and keep calm, never an easy thing to do at the best of times with my Mum but especially on a Monday morning when I'm running late.

"Mum, I'm up to date with the rent unless you are putting the rates up, and I don't think I am going into battle, though the way I am feeling it won't be long."

"Charge, Sarah, charge. You put the car battery on charge last night after flattening it yesterday."

"Oh my God," I thought out loud. She's right but I daren't admit it or I'll never hear the end of it. "I knew that Mum, I knew that, I just forgot for a split second or less."

Meekly I sloped off inside to disconnect the said battery on charge and reconnect my wonderful Boris to his supersonic self – well about 50mph downhill with the wind behind us anyway.

So, it was Monday, I was late, I was oily, large hole in my tights and a dried milk stain down my front. What else could a young teacher want? If only I knew what was in store for me I think I would have stayed in bed with Mr Snuggles – see book one before you get too excited or indignant.

I knew I was very late as soon as I turned into the school gates. There on the left side stone pillar was the sign of fresh metallic paint. It was a bright, purple colour and only my Year

33

4 colleague and Deputy Head, Mrs (Chlora) Form would be brave enough to drive a car of that awful shade. If she was in before me, it was the sign that I was mega-late and the time had turned past 8.30am. I parked Boris at record speed (for me) grabbed my bag and flung open the driver's door. For some unknown reason I glanced back at my beloved car, after about three strides I burst into tears. There was my pride and joy. There was my Boris with blacked out (oily) windows, mud covering all the underneath from my journey to the football match yesterday and on top of that he had now, apparently, been devalued by a tenth.

A week ago I had been persuaded at the end of a really good night out that I should play for the local ladies football team. I liked sport, I liked football but that didn't mean I was any good at it – in fact I was hopeless. But they were a friendly bunch of young single ladies aged between 17 and 24 and they gave me every encouragement. Unfortunately, that was not enough for me. Our games were nearly always on Sunday afternoons, home and away, and surprisingly we always had a large crowd of supporters to cheer us on for 90 minutes (apart from when they were laughing). But there was this thing that baffled me, nearly all of our band of supporters were young men!

Boris had a lovely black and white number 7 inside a circle on the side of the car on both front doors. Some of the black mud had splattered further up to create what at first glance looked like a decimal point to the left of the printed 7 – he was now 0.7. I flew up the driveway to my classroom with tears running off my face as if it was heavy rainfall.

I entered my classroom in tears. Little did I know that I would also leave it in tears at the end of the day. Bursting into my classroom I quickly inspected my bag that had been full of children's books to mark and assess over the weekend. It was then that I discovered there was one book missing, no not a child's but my diary. I must have left it at home. This act of forgetfulness can be disaster to a teacher. What am I doing today? Have I any meetings? Phone calls to make? Items to prepare for the weekly staff meeting? Even, more importantly, shopping!

Thank goodness it was no longer my playground duty before the start of school on a Monday morning. No longer was I the new girl on the block, the only Newly Qualified Teacher (NQT) in town. That honour now went to Maria Cheeseburger a lovely young lady but difficult to keep a straight face to when she was introduced to you for the first time. I just managed to get everything out in time for the children at the start of the school day/week. Fortunately for me my trusty new Teaching Assistant, Mrs Bull had arrived earlier than she really needed to or was paid for. Schools could not possibly operate without the goodwill and unpaid hours put in by most of its staff. The registers had been taken and the literacy lesson started when a grim faced Miss Steak entered my classroom. She was not alone. Mrs Form was also with her, a sight never seen before during lesson time in my room.

By the looks on their faces they were not about to start a double act of singing, dancing or telling jokes. Miss Steak came across and quietly told me that she needed to see me in her office immediately and the Deputy Head would be taking the rest of the lesson. This indeed was a serious matter, what had I done or what had I not done that I should have done by now? The walk behind my Headteacher seemed a long, lonely and scary one where the silence was deafening. We reached her office, THE OFFICE, and the door was closed.

"Please sit down Sarah, I need to talk." No she didn't need to talk, I thought to myself, she was a Headteacher they talk and talk at the drop of a hat. I think it must be a requirement and an integral part of their school interview that they talk for at least half an hour but manage to say absolutely nothing. They are experts, there should be a TV programme just for people like that. Oh I forgot there was, it was called 'Politics Today'.

However, this did not have the feel of one of those occasions.

"Amanda and Simon Hotspur, Sarah. How were they when they came into school this morning?"

"Fine, Miss Steak, fine."

I find myself choosing my words very carefully on the few occasions I have to join in a conversation with her. I have to try very hard to avoid using words like 'well done', 'medium' and 'rare'.

"They were a little bit flustered as their Mum and Dad were late for work and dropped them at the school gates just as the whistle blew for Key Stage 2 to line up. That is most unusual for them." I continued.

Miss Steak's face grew grimmer and at that moment she looked away from me and peered at the carpet space between us. "Sarah, half an hour after the start of school Mr and Mrs Hotspur were killed in a multiple car accident on the motorway."

Amanda and Simon were absolutely identical. This was probably something to do with the fact that they were twins. But this was unusual as they were, of course, brother and sister. One other most unusual fact about these two was that they were supposed to be in different school year groups. What! I hear you think, that's impossible. Well Amanda was born at 11.45pm on 31st August, Simon at 12.15am on 1st September. Officially the school year starts at midnight on 31st August or a second into 1st September. Over the years their family had experienced problems with some petty authorities and schools who were sticklers for the rules. A few (including ours I am pleased to say) could see it was plain common sense for them to be in the same academic year group. They were great kids, always bright and cheerful and often finished each other's sentences they were so tuned into one other. If we had a maths test and Amanda had 18 out of 20 then so did Simon. In spelling if Simon had a certain word spelt incorrectly then surprise, surprise so did Amanda, even though they sat well apart on different tables. Amanda and Simon were both good at sports and even though they had only been there a short time they had managed to land the school in trouble with competition and festival organisers on several occasions. In sports like tag rugby, kwik cricket or netball, mixed gender teams usually play and wore the same coloured school kit. Other schools often complained that we had too few girls or too many boys sometimes as they couldn't tell the difference between the two of them and always assumed they were the same gender.

After hearing this news I'm not sure how long the pause of silence lasted, it could have been brief or it could have been minutes, I simply haven't a clue. The next thing I did remember was that we were both in floods of tears and hugging each other. Just at that moment the door opened and Mrs Ored entered with a cup of tea for both of us. Barbara always knew when that special cup of tea was needed (like every good school secretary). This was the best cup of tea I had ever tasted; the fact that I don't actually drink tea probably had something to do with it. Months later, I discovered that she had also put a little bit of brandy into it. "Purely for medicinal purposes," she said, "for the shock of the occasion."

Following this miraculous cup of tea 'Jos', as I was now allowed to call our Headteacher, and I had our chat. No that was a poor description of how it went, I listened as Jos Steak spoke.

"Sarah, as you know the children only joined us two months ago after the family relocated to this area due to their mother's work, none of their relatives were within 150 miles of here and it will be quite a few hours before their Aunt Alice (the mother's sister) will be able to travel here, perhaps even the end of the school day. Their Aunt has said how happy the children have been at St Alemate's and that is mainly down to you and how much the twins respect you."

At this point, I started to build up a really strange feeling inside, my nerves were on edge, those butterfly things had taken flight inside my stomach and I started to squirm about on my chair.

"Sarah, the Aunt has asked that you be the one that breaks the news to them about their parents. I immediately said no to that, of course, and that it was completely out of the question and an unreasonable request to ask any teacher especially one so new to the job."

Phew! I thought, thanks for that one Jos.

"I then told their Aunt that it would have to be a task I did in such tragic circumstances. But the Aunt was very strong in her opinion, apparently she is in charge of a women's prison, telling me that the children could not possibly be told by me as they hated me and the only teacher that could tell them with any sensitivity and understanding was you, Sarah Ing."

Right on cue Mrs Ored arrived with a second round of teas. My Headteacher continued, as they do. "This has to be your decision Sarah. I cannot insist that you do this. I feel it is unfair on you and way beyond your expected job description." A pause followed.

"I'll do it Miss Steak," I blurted out just after swallowing the final mouthful of tea+. I'm not sure who was more surprised, my Headteacher or me. Mrs Form took my class for the remainder of the morning's lessons. After a frantic mid-morning break during which news of the tragic event started to spread around the staff, I had a long session talking with my new best friend Jos about how I was going to deal with this horrific event.

Midday supervisors (or dinner ladies) are amazing people. They do a difficult job really well and they know just about everything that goes on. I am sure that a lot of them could easily have trained as spies or undercover police during difficult times throughout our history. Mrs Cobb was one such lady, she looked too thin to be a Midday Supervisor and years ago, unknown to her, the older children had nicknamed her 'Skeletor' after a character in a TV programme.

Mrs Cobb casually walked up to me and asked if I had heard about the dreadful motorway accident that had killed two people. I suppose she didn't actually need an answer, the look of horror on my face must have given her all the answers she needed without posing a direct question. Obviously she didn't know their identities (yet) but had a reasonable idea that they might be from our area.

I didn't eat any lunch that day, just no appetite at all. However, I did make a point of going out into the playground just to see that the twins were their usual lively selves, and they were. At one point I was aware that Skeletor had her eye on me and I was worried that she might try to put two and two together but not arrive at the right answer.

Aunt Alice telephoned the school to say that she would not be able to arrive until around 4pm and please could I be with the children until she arrived. We decided (Jos and I) not to tell the twins until around 2.30pm. Their class would be changing after P.E. and just about to start some singing before story and the end of the school day.

The Deputy Head's room was empty, of course, as Chlora was teaching my class. Just before half past two I wandered down to my classroom to meet up with Amanda and Simon. Although I arrived there before half past two it was gone 2.35pm before I plucked up the courage to enter my own classroom. I had lost count of exactly how many times I nearly touched, brushed against or made contact with the door handle until I had enough strength to open it and my hand had started to shake a little less. Lots of children were milling about so it was easy for me to walk in there without being too much of a distraction.

Amanda was nearest and I easily made eye contact with her and signalled for her to come with me. Simon was a tougher prospect. He had his back to me and was chatting away with two of his friends. I gently tapped him on the shoulder, on that touch he spun round and said, "Hello Miss Ing, you've been missing Miss Ing, where've you been then, not skiving I hope?"

I smiled, well I tried my best to, what exactly came out I will probably never know. He also followed me out across the classroom, Mrs Form gave me a knowing but very sympathetic look along with a little wave as I crossed over the room. We walked down the corridor to the Deputy's room, well I walked, the twins bounced, "Really missed you today Miss," said Amanda.

I had rearranged Mrs Form's room with three comfortable chairs in a sort of equilateral triangle shape. Honestly, I cannot remember the exact words I used to tell them. It is something I had gone over dozens of times in my head over the past few hours. I knew what I had planned to say but what came out at the saddest moment of my life so far was a mystery. One thing I knew for sure was that we all cried and we all hugged in our triangle of emotion. We must have kept in that same position, that shape of strength, for some time. The next thing I remembered was the sound of children making their way home and Mrs Ored entering with biscuits, orange squash and my special tea.

Between three and four o'clock we didn't say much, there was a lot of eye contact between the three of us, lots of tears and quite a few more hugs. At some point Miss Steak, Mrs Form and Mrs Ored all entered the room briefly. No one spoke, no one smiled, no one even exchanged glances.

41

Just after four the door opened again and in stepped Aunt Alice. Immediately the children both ran to her. They flung their arms partly around her ample waist and they let the tears flow once more. After a few minutes Aunt Alice reached across in my direction, looked me straight in the face and silently said, 'Thank you'.

Mrs Form crept in with the twin's bags, coats and lunchboxes and exited without saying a word. Just as she closed the door I started to follow her but was stopped by a trio of voices asking me not to leave but to come back to the house. This took me by surprise and I told them I would have to ask permission first as it was now time for our weekly staff meeting. This was a meeting where it was frowned upon if you dared to miss it. Aunt Alice was there before me and by the time I reached the Head's office permission had been granted and all the necessary arrangements made. The prison governess drove and after Mrs Ored's special teas, it was probably just as well.

Aunt Alice had a key to the door, how she had one I just don't know and I certainly wasn't about to ask. Just inside the front door and Alice froze to the spot apparently in fear. Heading straight down the hallway towards her was a beautiful yellow Labrador dog, fully grown and extremely lively, "How long have you had THAT?" shouted Aunt Alice.

"Only about a month Auntie, didn't you know?" replied Amanda.

By this time Aunt Alice had started to sneeze, sniff, shake, cough and …

"Oh!" said Simon, "Of course, you're allergic to cats and dogs. I'd forgotten about that."

"Out! Out!" screamed Aunt Alice. "He will have to go, he can't live with me."

The twins looked at each other and then at the dog. Alfie the Labrador had one of those faces that told you exactly how he felt; he had eyes that spoke volumes. By now he had the saddest face I had ever seen on any animal. He knew something was wrong, he didn't know what or why, Alfie just knew that things were not as they should be. With his head flat on the ground, paw on either side of his mouth, the word SADNESS was written all over his face in bold capital letters.

The twins decided that in the circumstances the best course of action was to take Alfie for a walk. Shortly after the dog was out of the house, Aunt Alice seemed about normal (ish). She had her deeply, deeply worried face on and pointed it straight in my direction. "Miss Ing, what am I to do?"

"Please call me Sarah," I replied, but that was all I could think to say at the moment. I knew what she was thinking, but answers, I had none.

She disappeared upstairs and was clattering about for around 20 minutes. During this time the children and Alfie all returned and were playing in the back garden, the three of them felt safer there. "Miss Ing?" the twins chorused, "We won't be able to stay," continued Amanda. "Aunt Alice has her job and family at the other end of the country," continued Simon.

"Miss Ing?" added Amanda.

"Yes, Amanda," I replied.

"Please can you take care of Alfie for us? We've been talking and we know there's no way Auntie can have him as well. She wouldn't even be able to drive with the dog in the car."

"We collected him from an animal shelter," said Simon, "we couldn't let him go back there. When we first got him you could see every rib on his body and he had fleas."

"I really don't know children," I said, "I live at home with my parents..."

On that word I stopped, my heart sank, my mouth dried and I melted inside.

"Yes, of course I will children. I would love to have Alfie and you can come and visit him anytime you're in the area."

The children cheered and a rather surprised Aunt arrived at the back door but ventured no further. By the time her foot was on the doorstep she knew what had been decided. However, inside my head there were little voices shouting, "You're mad", and, "What will your mother say?" plus, "You haven't got time to look after a dog!"

I knew that but I was determined that I was going to make it work – for the twin's sake. After that day I never saw them again, they wrote to the class a few times and emailed me twice, but that was all.

Meanwhile, there I was heading back home, eventually, bringing back rather more than I had left with that morning. Jos kindly came out to the house after the staff meeting to give me a lift back to school. I could tell that she was less than impressed to be returning with two passengers in her car, one of them canine. My Mum kept a really tidy house and had often said that one of the reasons it was so neat was because we had no pets. So what kind of reception was I going to receive when I arrived home and just how much rent was a place of my own?

CHAPTER FOUR

IN THE DOG HOUSE WITH A COLD SHOULDER

It seemed a long drive home that evening, on a day I would always remember. A tragic memory that will probably bring tears to my eyes for the rest of my life. Boris (my loyal 2CV) seemed reluctant to travel much above 30mph and my additional passenger was sitting on the seat next to me with sad eyes staring up at me as if to say, 'What now Sarah, what now?'

I really should have phoned my Mum to let her know that I would be late for tea and warn her about Alfie. It might have been easier on the phone but to be honest what would I say, how could I have explained the events of today and why that now included a dog in my life? On my arrival at home, I turned off the engine and just sat there feeling numb. After a while, I turned to Alfie and asked him what he thought and how to best deal with the tricky situation of walking into a house where he would almost certainly receive a hostile welcome. Unfortunately, Alfie was not in a chatty mood and played the strong, silent, male role on this occasion.

Alfie

About thirty minutes later I plucked up enough courage to go inside along with my four legged bodyguard. We were only a few steps inside the front door when Mum appeared in the hallway. Her first expression was one of annoyance at how late I was, but then she spotted the dog. It was amazing how many different ways a mother can say a simple two letter word. I can certainly remember it said with a wide variety of tone, expression, stresses and volume. The 'no' sentences were ended by the word, 'never!' I tried to speak but I had no chance, my Dad appeared in the background and also tried to force a word in but without success. After the word, 'never' came out, Alfie was the first to do a u turn and made back towards the front door. It really was a shame that she didn't give me a chance to fully (or partly) explain the circumstances though I was not exactly sure how I would have said it.

The three of us tried to settle down for the night on the driveway (Boris, Alfie and me). Perhaps I could try again in the morning if my Mum would let me through the front door? After a search around the car boot I found some blankets and an old coat that could act as a pillow. So with a heavy heart, an empty stomach and a cold wet nose we settled down for the night. The back seat of a Citroen 2CV was obviously never designed to be laid out on. With a combination of all the seat belt attachments and the normal curves and bumps, it felt like laying down on a cobbled beach in Sussex.

After about an hour, (that felt like three) there was a knocking noise. Now, if we had been travelling on the journey to and from school I wouldn't have thought any more about it, but of course the car engine was off. The noise kept on and became louder and when I sat up there was a face looking through the window at me. I screamed at the top of my voice and Alfie barked with all his might and the shape that was my Dad ran away quicker than I had seen him move for about a decade.

Very slowly he returned to the car waving his arms above his head as if to surrender. I opened the car door to let him in. Dad sat on the driver's seat and calmly told me that about half an hour ago Miss Steak had phoned to ask how I was. She had been trying my mobile phone but, I realised now, it was asleep in my desk drawer at school so there had been no answer. There then followed a thirty minute conversation between my Headteacher and my Mum when everything had been explained. Apparently, Miss Steak had said how proud she was of me in the difficult circumstances and hoped I could get a good night's sleep.

This, of course, made my Mum feel really guilty and she had sent Dad out to apologise and get me back into the house … and the dog, but he had to sleep in the conservatory tonight (Alfie, not my Dad on this occasion). My re-re-heated meal still tasted good and there was even enough for Alfie, but don't tell my Mother!

The next morning at breakfast there was an uneasy truce. Mum was obviously proud about what she had heard from my Headteacher but every few minutes she would shoot a glare in the direction of Alfie. Dad had been next door to borrow some dog food and in return the dog had shown his appreciation by creating a large, brown, pointed, squidgy, statue creation in the middle of the lawn, as well as lifting his leg and watering Mum's favourite rose bush. I went upstairs to collect everything for school only to find that Alfie had been shut up in the conservatory on his own by the time I returned. This was not going to be easy, I thought to myself. Alfie would have to come to school with me and stay in the car until I could make some better arrangements.

There was a very strange atmosphere at school that day, only half my class turned up due to children being too upset after finding out the full tragic story about their classmates' family. They were even more upset when I told them that they had now left the school for ever. We never actually saw the twins again; they just disappeared with their Aunt. However, I did receive a long email from them about a week later telling me about their new school, home and friends. Sadly, they didn't ask after Alfie.

CHAPTER FIVE

NO PLACE LIKE HOME

I had to leave home. It was a 'no brainer' of a decision – a phrase someone once said to me. For everyone's sake, finding my own place to live with Alfie was essential for all concerned. After all, I had lived here for 23 years so perhaps it was time to give my Mum and Dad a break.

I contacted all the estate agents in town and scoured through the local newspapers to compile a list of my next possible residence. After working out the finance side of things, my long list was reduced from 70 to 32. Putting the Alfie factor into the equation as well now left a short list of … four! The words 'No pets' were printed on most of the details. Everyone tells me we are a nation of animal lovers. I think that should read that we are a nation of pet lovers if you don't include the people who own property to rent.

So my short list of four included two flats and two apartments. What strange words to use describing a place to live. There was no way that a building was 'flat'. How on earth did it come to be called that? Apartments were usually small places that are joined on to each other so the last thing they

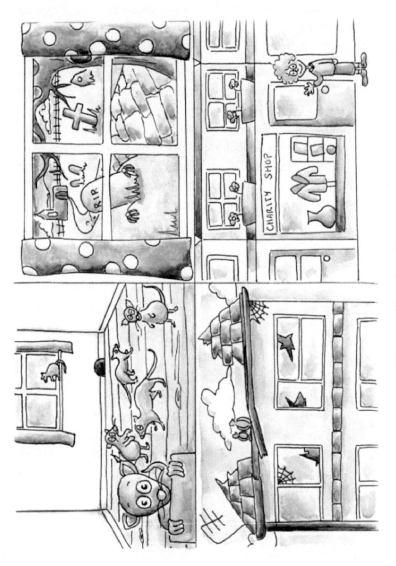

House Hunting Horrors

were was 'apart'. English was such an odd language sometimes.

On the Friday evening I closely studied my short list of four like a Headteacher looking at application forms for a job at school. One was described as, 'In need of love and attention'. Well I could do that, no problem. The second was, 'ideally situated for all amenities'. Number three was, 'available for use immediately', and the last one was described as having, 'the view of a lifetime!' They were all in different parts of town so I planned a running order to visit them at the weekend and contacted the three agents.

My Friday night in the conservatory was one that brought very little sleep. A mixture of excitement at the very thought of my own first place and the task of comforting a crying, howling, restless Labrador easily saw to that. About half an hour after we had nodded off, up rose the sun to light up an east facing row of windows into my new, very temporary bedroom. Well, at least it left me plenty of time to shower, get dressed, breakfast, feed and walk the dog. In fact I still had two hours to spare having completed that list quite slowly. Mum and Dad were also up surprisingly early for a Saturday. Apparently they thought that they would come with Alfie and me to look at the properties. Now this was such a moment where parents often go wrong with their children. They assumed something was going to happen but hadn't actually asked about it. Ooops!

Alfie and I left alone. Well we were together but just the two of us if you know what I mean. First on our list was number 3 'available for use immediately': oh yes please, I thought, as we drove towards the attached apartment. It was a ground floor place next to an empty field. I opened the door and my every sound echoed around as did the noise of my dog on the uncarpeted floor. Alfie looked around the two back rooms and I inspected the front. So far so good. I had nearly completed my look around the first place when the dog arrived back and lay down flat at my feet. Alfie never did this even in his training, this was a first!

Just after he lay down at my ankles, I could still hear the echo of feet moving around in the building. They were quick moving, scratching, scurrying type feet. I looked at the second room and then ventured into Alfie's early discovery. At first glance everything looked fine, large room, decorated, clean but infested with rats. This place was already occupied. One down and three to go.

Number 2 was a flat on the edge of town close to the church and local primary school. It was the fourth on my list and apparently had the, 'view of a lifetime'. After looking all around the place I could see what they meant. The back two rooms both had a perfect view of the cemetery, lovely flowers, no late night parties (apart from Hallowe'en) and a view to die for but sorry, not for me. Alfie did hint at something about bones but I just ignored him.

My third choice, Number 1, said to be, 'in need of love and attention'. On arriving outside we took one look and accelerated rapidly – well as rapidly as a 2CV is capable of anyway. Love and attention was one thing but there was no mention of the missing roof in the flat details.

So three down, just one to go and I was feeling rather low. The final one had an address on the High Street, a place I had walked down many times but never seen homes to actually live in. On arriving there I realised why. The apartment was above one of the shops. It was a charity shop owned by a local trust. The lady was very welcoming and she even had a biscuit for Alfie so that convinced him before we had even seen the place. All four rooms were quite large, clean, decorated and rodent free. It was empty at the moment and it met my price range so I thanked the manager and hurried off to the agent to start filling in the forms. After explaining my circumstances, he said that if the bank and other references could be completed very quickly the place would be mine by the following weekend.

It wasn't easy to make sure my bank, my Headteacher and my Local Authority salaries department had completed all the required forms in five days but after a lot of phone calls, mileage and gifts of cream cakes on my part, it was done. Some furniture had been left by the previous tenants, my parents allowed me to take the items from my own bedroom plus a spare settee. So with a few friends from the ladies football team and two of their boyfriends, plus a work's van, it only took a few hours to move in. By five o'clock on the Saturday we were in and alone, by six I had a takeaway from three doors down and by seven I realised that we had no electricity or gas because I had forgotten to contact the agencies about having it reconnected. So much for lists!

I briefly thought about going home but decided in the circumstances it was probably best not to on my very first night. Alfie and I would just have to be brave and then buy some candles and a torch tomorrow as it would probably not be possible to speak to a human voice until Monday morning.

Opening all the curtains was a good move, so that I could see most of the room with the lights from the High Street and car headlights pausing at regular intervals. It was enough for me to make the bed and sort a lot of things out for now. By

8.30pm everything was sorted but with no electricity, no gas, no TV, no music centre, no radio, no games station and not a lot of sleep the previous night finally decided it – an early bed. With a football match in the morning playing against the top of the table and closest rivals Barfchester Untidy, I needed all the rest I could get.

Falling asleep was easy. So was the waking up. The only problem was it was still Saturday, late on but not yet midnight. It sounded like one group was practising for the church choir but singing badly out of tune and not all using the same words at the same time. They must have come out of my now local pub across the road, 'The Ball and Chain'. Fortunately for everyone, they gradually faded into the distance. Unfortunately for me, I couldn't get to sleep again for hours. Just lying there and trying really hard to go to sleep was probably the worst thing you could do. Especially, when my imagination kicked in and the least sound was magnified in the darkness with numerous noises, bangs, clatters, bumps, rattles and others that I couldn't identify. Half an hour later of deliberately listening out for these sounds and I was starting to convince myself that my new home was actually haunted or infested. Then a new noise, a moaning, groaning throaty sound that went up and down. Most worrying was the fact that it sounded very close,

Miss Ing Header

then I realised it was the dog dreaming, snoring and probably chasing a rabbit. Well, at least one of us was asleep.

Early morning arrived far too soon for my sleep pattern but there were many things to do before leaving in Boris, collecting two other members of the team and heading down the road towards Barfchester. Alfie needed feeding, walking and an opportunity to raise one of his back legs – poor tree. Kit sorted and packed after breakfast and we were off. I stopped a mile away on the other side of town to collect Sammy and Danni from their semi-detached house.

Our game against Barfchester Untidy was an unusual one to say the least. We lost 4-3 and somehow I managed to score three goals (a hat-trick). My first was when I crossed the ball from the side aiming for Sammy and the ball sailed over their goalkeeper. The second was a header, I suppose, as I was walking back away from their goal, the goalkeeper kicked the ball from her hands against the back of my head and it rebounded into the net. My third was an attempted shot at the goal but I completely miskicked it and after hitting the referee on his bottom it sent the goalie the wrong way and trickled over the line. Our group of young lads had grown in recent weeks and they cheered most of my goals after they had finished laughing out loud. Their strange attempts at singing and chanting football tunes had a familiar ring to it but I couldn't think where I had heard it before. Still, a 4-3 defeat was a good result against the unbeaten Barfchester and we remained in third place. The updated goal scorers list showed me on top spot after that game, just two goals ahead of someone called OG. Not sure about her first name or even what she looked like. A quick fruit juice and a bite to eat at their village pub and then it was back to my new home with

Alfie, a pile of maths books to mark and my lesson planning for the week ahead while it was still daylight.

The next week simply flew by with all my school work and the forward planning for our next annual residential week down on the farm. Dashing home every lunchtime to let Alfie out was a bit of a nuisance but I couldn't keep him stuck in the car all day. Suddenly, it was Friday again and back to my upstairs apartment for the next weekend. But at least there would be electricity and gas for this one.

CHAPTER SIX

FORGET FRIDAY THE 14TH
(teachers love alliteration)

Friday evenings for a lot of people my age were nights out, perhaps a drink or three and socialising, but not for me. I usually tried to complete all my school work of marking, planning and assessments to leave Saturday and Sunday clear to relax a little and recharge my batteries for the next week. Teaching can be quite an exhausting occupation and I can fully sympathise with actors as we both perform for hours each day in front of an audience, usually very enjoyable and rewarding but occasionally disaster can strike. It could be mechanical or you forget your lines, at such times you need to improvise, think on your feet or risk a performance that the audience will remember for a long time and tell all their friends.

The evening of Friday the 14th was following the same pattern as the previous three Fridays of the term, Alfie walked and fed, marking up to date, planning finished so I could reward myself with an evening meal and a few hours television before bed. Approaching midnight I felt relaxed enough to turn in for a good night's rest with no alarm clock to disturb me and if I could manage to keep my eyes closed with my beloved dog centimetres away from rubbing noses in the hope of an early breakfast, I just might have a little lie in.

The male voice choir of the Ball and Chain had earlier been practising their full repertoire of songs with no signs of improvement since I'd heard them that first time. To be honest, I think they were getting worse! As I stood up to head for the bathroom I gave a casual glance down to the High Street pavement from my upstairs viewpoint. A strange sight caught my attention. In the doorway of the mobile phone shop there was the shadowy figure of what looked like a young man. His movements were abnormal and my glance turned into a stare. He briefly held onto the frame of the shop entrance before sinking to his knees. I suppose he could be at prayer, I thought naïvely, or looking for something he had dropped. After a short while, he staggered to his feet in a standing, leaning pose, propping up the doorway just in case it fell down. A few moments later he left this safety spot and stepped back out onto the High Street, five steps later he fell over as if he had trodden on his shoelaces. It had the same effect as pulling hard on just the front brake of your bicycle, his head hit the pavement face down and there he lay, motionless!

Now what? Do I just ignore him and go to bed? Do I dial 999? I decided to go to the bathroom, clean my teeth and perhaps by the time I returned he would have gone... somewhere, anywhere out of my line of vision and thoughts would be great. What was that saying Mum often recited, 'out of sight, out of mind'. At this moment in time, I would settle for that.

On my slower than usual return to the living room, I almost had my eyes closed, hoping and praying that the kisser of pavements would have gone. A swift glance out of the window lifted my hopes. But a closer look dashed them – the shadowy floor figure remained. Right, so on to Plan B then, whatever it was. How brave or foolish was I feeling? I rang my friend Susan who lived quite near so that we could go down there together – no reply apart from that annoying, pre-recorded, computerised, voicemail. I had to do something, he could have been taken ill, be dying or badly injured and in need of hospital care.

Alfie had settled himself down for the night and was in a deep and active dream of chasing something. His feet were running, though he was flat on his side, the tail was pounding on the floor and his mouth was making a muffled woof of excitement and anticipation. My disturbing his make-believe chase of a lifetime did not go down too well. He knew his evening walk had been and gone, the chances of him being taken on a second one at this time of night were less than zero. So the sound of me picking up his lead that usually turned him wild with excitement meant nothing this time, not even a second glance. However, the smell and appearance of his favourite biscuit treat was another story and a sure-fire way to rouse him from doggy slumber land.

As we set foot on the pavement across the road from the mobile phone shop there was an eerie silence up and down the High Street. We crossed over with me firmly in second place, Alfie seeming keen to investigate the pile of clothes on the pavement. He started under its armpit area and worked his way up to the head. Despite a severe licking of the face and a cold

Rocky Cliff

wet nose across the cheek there was no movement from the pile of jumble still sniffing out the paving slabs. However, the after-effects of the biscuits had not yet worn off, a combination of his slobber and the saliva dripping out of Alfie's mouth ran into the man's ear. After the hole was full to capacity, the overflow ran across his cheek and dripped inside his partly opened lips. This seemed to do the trick and after a few licks of the lips a groaning noise answered at least one of my questions – he wasn't dead!

Following a few moans, groans, coughs, splutters and ridding himself of Alfie's resuscitation fluid he sat himself up against the shop window. It wasn't until then that I noticed he was carrying a sports bag with the name Cliff Link written on it and a badge style symbol emblazoned above the words. The name sounded familiar but I couldn't think why. At that moment he started to talk, muttering about something he had eaten making him feel unwell, but the blood from his nose was trickling down into his mouth and a large lump was appearing in the middle of his forehead. His words were slurred, sounding similar to my Grandad a few years ago when I went to visit him just after he had suffered a stroke.

I decided, rightly or wrongly, that he needed a Good Samaritan and as there was no one else in sight, I had been nominated. After helping him to stand, we all crossed the road and slowly started to make our way up the stairs. When I say we, I mean all three of us, I don't think it would have been possible if I hadn't tied Alfie's lead to his right wrist and he helped pull him up the steps to my apartment. We put him on the settee and I tidied up the mess that was once his face. Alfie and I went to get him a drink of water but by the time I returned he was fast asleep, clutching his sports bag firmly to his chest with both hands. Cliff Link's face definitely looked familiar, but I couldn't place it and I went to bed still wondering where I had seen him.

Three or four hours later, I woke up and thought I'd better check on the health of my unexpected visitor. On walking into the living room it was quite a shock to find an empty settee. Had he just left without saying a word? Been abducted by aliens? Was it all a dream? Alfie had decided to join me on my early-morning stroll but had then headed off towards the bathroom. Catching him up, I could see why, there was my guest fast asleep in the bath, still holding tight to that bag. It must be something very valuable in there. Feeling concerned for my unwanted but needy visitor I put the toilet lid down onto the seat and sat down to monitor Mr Link for a few minutes.

Four hours later, I awoke in a crumpled up shape, feeling rather uncomfortable and stiff necked, but with feet as warm as toast. Glancing down, I could see that Alfie had spread himself all across my bare feet in his best effort to help me out. My hero! I wasn't sure what time it was by then, but daylight was breaking through and I was awake so the churning noises coming from the stomach area of my fur coated hero and best friend certainly said to one of us that it was time for breakfast. After Alfie had devoured his bowl of food, (Labradors don't eat daintily and only at one speed… FULL!) If he hadn't already been named, I think I would have called him 'Dyson' for the way he hoovers up anything edible in and around his path. Being in an upstairs apartment I couldn't just let the dog out, he always had to be taken. So loaded up with 'poo bags', his favourite treats and a ball we set off for our morning walk. I checked on Sleeping Beauty just before I left, he was in a deep snooze with his head placed neatly between the hot and cold taps and his right leg hanging over the side of the bath.

About 45 minutes later, Alfie and I returned, the dog weighing quite a lot less than when we set off. As usual I took off his lead as soon as we were through the door and without hesitation he ran to the bathroom, put his paws on the shoulders of my guest and licked him straight across the mouth, nose and cheek. It's a good job he hadn't seen where Alfie had his tongue a few minutes earlier, after bending his body around into an oval shaped canine to do it. Cliff Link woke up in a rush. After this warm embrace, he banged both sides of his head on the taps, sat bolt upright, looking straight at me and uttered one word, "Gazza!"

I was rather taken aback by this short sentence. It wasn't the first time I had heard it shouted though. This word was often being chanted on a Sunday afternoon during matches played by my ladies football team, Albion Myway. I briefly explained to an embarrassed Cliff what had happened the previous night and how he had ended up sleeping in my bath. After leaving him to sort himself out, I went into the kitchen to make some breakfast with strong coffee top of the list. About 10 minutes later, a shy Mr Link slowly walked into the kitchen and sat down. He looked very much like one of the children from my class who knew they had done something wrong and were waiting for the verbal telling off.

I served him with an excellent breakfast of black coffee, cereal, toast, yoghurt and more black coffee. He gave me the impression that none of these would have been on his chosen menu but in the circumstances he thought it best to do as he was told – how wise! His feeble explanation was that he had stepped outside the Ball and Chain for a cigarette with one of his friends. He remembered chatting to him while they were stood in 'Cancer Corner', his next memory was being given mouth-to-mouth resuscitation by a large dog with very bad breath. He couldn't stop apologising and said it must have been something that he had eaten that had made him ill. He also asked if he could thank me by taking me out for a meal. Perhaps I was rather unkind to reply that I didn't want to eat at the places he visited if it made him that ill and that in any case I wouldn't want to go out anywhere with a walking, talking ashtray.

Silence reigned for the next few minutes until I broke it by asking him why he uttered the word Gazza on first opening his eyes this morning. After taking another gulp of his coffee he explained that he, along with his so-called friends, often watched my ladies football team try to play football on Sundays. One of his group thought I looked a bit like a gazelle, lovely long legs, graceful in movement, but didn't use its head. I was more than happy with his explanation until the final few words, I think he was expecting me to laugh or smile, but he received neither. A few more minutes of silence followed. Then I noticed the look of horror on his face as he glanced up at my kitchen clock, "Is that time correct?" he asked.

"No," I replied, much to his initial relief, "it's an hour slow, I forgot to change it last weekend when the time moved on an extra 60 minutes."

His early feeling of relief dramatically changed back to horror and then moved on to severe fear mixed with panic. I asked if he had a problem and perhaps he was late for meeting his girlfriend. His complexion was pale anyway after the events of last night and it now turned to a brilliant gloss shade of white terror, "I'll miss the coach," he choked out, "the manager will kill me, I'll be sacked, transferred or worse," he continued.

"What coach?" I enquired innocently.

"The coach to Downtown City!" he snapped back.

At this I left him to stew in his own mess up and cleared away the breakfast dishes, plates and cups. I could hear him frantically making several phone calls on his mobile. But when I returned the look of panic on his face had not yet subsided. "Gazza," he said softly, "any chance you could give me a lift to Downtown City's ground? I am in big trouble already and I don't know what to do, I'll gladly pay your petrol."

I cleared away the rest of the items on the kitchen table and put them away in various cupboards. "Gazza?" I heard again, it was starting to annoy me.

"Look!" I snapped back, "my name is Sarah, not Gazza. Why should I drive you, a stranger, to Downtown City? That's a two hour journey each way and a large part of my day off used up."

At the gradual raising of my voice, Alfie had woken from his chase and was standing between Mr Link and me staring at him in as threatening a way as a Labrador can possibly look. Cliff sank back down in his chair, put his head in his hands and fell down a well of despair. I tried to ease his pain by saying that as a football supporter it didn't really matter if he was there or not to support his team. He then said words that made his urgency far more real, "I'm not a supporter Sarah. I play for Mancpool Rovers, I'm their striker and current top scorer."

CHAPTER SEVEN

BORIS TO THE RESCUE – AT TOP SPEED

Now the penny dropped inside my head. That was where I had seen him before, in the newspaper and the television sports' programmes. Though I have to say it was not always on the back pages where all the football was reported, sometimes it was on the inside or even the front page as he had a bit of a bad boy reputation. He had the reputation as a wild man, untamed and simply bad news, with a number of nicknames, never mind making one up for me. Despite being in his early 20s, he had already been at several professional football clubs, including one in the Premiership but they had all transferred him on after a season or less, and now he was at our local club, who were in the Championship at the moment after being relegated about three seasons ago. Mancpool were now in a play-off place with about five or six league games to go. Downtown City was a crucial game, I had heard people say. "Why do people say you have had more clubs than Rory McIlroy?" I asked.

"What?" he replied, looking up at me with what appeared to be tears in his eyes, "What sort of question is that?"

"A truthful one," I added, "come on, grab your things. You can think of an answer on the way to Downtown City."

As we headed south on our journey, Cliff did most of the talking as he tried to explain all the nicknames that he had. Apparently most professional footballers have them, sometimes they just added the letter Y onto their surname or call them by a girl's first name that is similar to the one they already have. At each club on his way up to the Premiership he had collected quite a few. Early on he was called 'Cuff Link' instead of Cliff, at another it was 'Jailer' as his name was C Link and clink was a slang term for a prison. He had actually played for a season with today's opponents when they were in the Premiership and there he was called 'Rhino'. I didn't understand this one, but Cliff's problem seemed to be against figures of authority like the referee. Every decision that went against him or his team was wrong, in his opinion, and he argued, shouted, pointed and showed dissent against the officials. This had given him a bad reputation with the F.A. (Football Association) as he was booked and sent off a record number of times in one season. Rhino came about because he was always being 'charged' by the F.A.

Boris was doing his best to get there quickly and at one point on the motorway he actually touched 60mph. Cliff was becoming more and more restless as the number of cars that past us increased. He asked if he could smoke a cigarette and was firmly told NO! In fact, I took the pack off him to put temptation out of his way. To take his mind off what lay in store for him from his manager when he arrived at the ground, Alfie whispered sweet nothings in his ear and licked the back of his head from his place sat down on the backseat.

When we arrived at the ground, it was still over two hours to kick-off but the place was busy. Scarf-wearing fans from both teams were milling about outside waiting for the time they were allowed into the ground. Cliff pointed to the main entrance that said, 'Officials, Players and Directors only'. A large man in a uniform stopped me but after glancing across and recognising my passenger, he waved me in with a smirk across his face. Cliff grabbed his sports bag, shouted, "Thank you", and ran off. I turned the car around at the end of the car park and headed out. Just as I reached the main entrance again a suicidal idiot jumped out in front of me – it was Cliff. He opened the door and asked if I wanted to stay and watch the game, he had free tickets. I said, "No thank you, too busy, bye," and drove off past a sad faced looking, very late arriving, unprofessional footballer.

On the journey back, Alfie took his rightful place on the passenger seat at the front and sat up looking out of the windscreen. When Cliff exited the car, I didn't tell him that the seat of his trousers was plastered in blond dog's hair. I thought he had enough problems to sort out. Later, I switched the car radio on and tuned into the news and sports channel. It was being reported that star striker of Mancpool Rovers had been dropped from the team for today's game for disciplinary reasons but that he was named on the list of five substitutes.

By the time I arrived home, walked the dog, put the kettle on for a cup of tea and turned on the radio it was half-time in the game and Downtown were two goals up. But at the start of the second half, Mancpool brought on two substitutes and one of them was Cliff. When introduced to the crowd, he was loudly cheered by his own section of supporters, but their noise was drowned out by the jeering of the home town fans as they saw him as a danger and an ex-player who only stayed with them for one season. According to the radio commentator, Cliff had a few good passes and touches near the start of the second half. Then, after receiving the ball just outside the Downtown penalty area, he was flattened by the home team central defender known as The Hulk and Cliff was chewing mud. From the free-kick, their Russian winger Alexander Flukeov, slotted the ball into the top corner to make the score 2-1. With 20 minutes to go, Cliff took control of the ball about 40 metres out, passed the ball through The Hulk's wide open legs (why do they call that a nutmeg?) ran around him and scored the equaliser. With the full-time whistle 2 minutes away, a Mancpool corner led to Cliff heading the winning goal. Not that he knew anything much about it. As the ball hit his forehead, both the goalkeeper's fists landed on his chin and knocked him out. An unconscious Cliff Link was stretchered off to the dressing room passing the screaming Mancpool fans who were chanting his name. I have to admit it, I was slightly worried about him, but there was little I could do about it. I had no phone number or any contact details and he was getting used to sleeping in unusual places this weekend.

About five hours later, there was a knock at my door. This was very unusual at such a late hour. If my parents or friends called round they usually rang me first to make sure I was in. Alfie barked his way down the stairs to the door and I opened it to find the biggest bunch of flowers I had ever seen, plus a large box of chocolates on one side and a bottle of wine on the other. All these were supported by a pair of legs wearing trousers covered in blond dog hair. "Hello Cliff," I said, "come on in."

"How did you know it was me?" he replied, "what gave me away?"

I didn't have the heart to tell him. I think he was both surprised and impressed that I knew what had happened in the game and the final score. This, of course, was more than he knew until about half an hour after the match. The flowers were amazing and I quickly arranged them into two vases. We opened the chocolates, put the wine in the fridge and I made us both a cup of tea. We talked for hours as Cliff wanted to know about the gaps he had in his memory of the weekend so far. Later, we watched Match of the Day (a tune I now knew well), first game on was Downtown versus Mancpool so at least he saw his headed goal hit the net. After the game he was interviewed and to my astonishment, he told the commentator that he had been taken ill the evening before, (yeah, right) and that he dedicated his winning goal to Gazza, his Florence Nightingale. I think I went red.

After the programme I gave him a lift home, it was about 20 minutes away. He said he would see me tomorrow as he was coming to watch me play in our crucial league game against Kneely There Town.

CHAPTER EIGHT

SUPER SUNDAY

After such a hectic Saturday, I thought a Sunday morning lie in would be a good idea. Sadly, Alfie had other ideas. Animals often had this internal alarm clock that went off when it was time for important things in their lives, like food and walks. Monday to Friday I'm always up by 6:30am and he is fed by 7 and walked at 7:30am, I just fit in all my own preparations during the gaps. Alfie doesn't have to stay in the flat any more when I'm at school. I drop him off at a friend of my Mum's. She loves dogs, but hers died last year and she didn't want to start again with another new one. Having my dog during the day was just enough for her and they were good company for each other.

But today it was the weekend so up I rose, fed and walked him then went back to bed and everyone was happy. Later I had a light breakfast, not wanting to eat too much before a big match, and sorted out my sports kit for the afternoon game. I wondered if Cliff might call in to see me before the match but he didn't. Kneely There Town were top of the league, five points clear of anyone now and undefeated. To be honest, we just hoped to avoid being thrashed and keep the goals against in single figures.

Our team gradually arrived at the ground in ones and twos while Kneely There turned up in a 57 seater coach with their team and about 30 supporters making a lot of noise. They even cheered their team during the warm-up and clapped them onto the field for the start of the match. We just had Alfie barking his encouragement. Then right on the whistle to kick-off, the visiting fans were drowned out by a rousing chorus of "Gazza, Gazza, Gazza. Oi, Oi, Oi!" How embarrassing, it was Cliff and about 10 of his mates shouting support at the tops of their voices. At half-time it was still 0-0, I'm really not sure how, we were lucky to be nil. Their goalkeeper hadn't touched the ball once, Kneely There had hit both our posts, the crossbar twice, had two goals ruled offside, we cleared the ball off our line 3 times, twice they went round our goalkeeper only to miss an open goal and once their own player was in the way and the ball hit her just as it was about to cross the line. Still, as our manager Lou Cheyne, told us at half-time, "We are level and still have a chance. It's 11 v 11."

The second half continued in a similar vein, with us very much on the back foot (or was that feet). Both sets of fans continued to cheer although the Kneely There Town fans seemed to groan as much as cheer as yet another goalscoring chance went begging. Cliff's choir seemed to be decreasing in volume as some began to lose their voices. Ten minutes from the end, our luck finally ran out and they took the lead after their centre forward struck a fierce shot that hit the inside of our left hand goalpost, rebounded over our goalkeeper's head, hit the other post, then our goalie's face as she turned towards the ball and it landed in the back of the net. I touched the ball twice in the game. Once at the kick-off to start the second half and again after we conceded a goal.

As we trooped off at the end of the match Cliff met me, put his arm around my shoulder to say bad luck and asked if he could buy me an orange juice after I'd got changed. Bad luck I thought, from the two teams competing out there we had come a close third, but yes I will have the drink. Both teams of players and supporters stayed for about an hour at our local pub the 'First Inn Last Out', talking and laughing about the game.

After that, we all went our different ways, Cliff and I exchanged mobile phone numbers and he thanked me once more for what I had done on Saturday. Apparently, he had to report for extra training early on Monday morning as part of his punishment for being a naughty boy and arriving late on match day. We had our parents' evening next week and I had to make sure that all my marking and assessments were up to date, so no television for me that night – again!

CHAPTER NINE
THE MISSING LINK

Weekly staff meetings are an essential part of teaching life, though often they can be a tedious one. It only takes one member of staff to start yawning, even a little sneaky 'thought I'd disguised it really well' one and it immediately has the domino effect. Jaws were dropping. Eyes were rolling, watering and soon gradually closing. At the end of a hard day's teaching the last thing you wanted was an hour and a half, curriculum heavy meeting in a warm, stuffy room. No wonder there were so few questions, queries, challenges or disagreements from the vast majority of teachers, especially towards the end of the meeting. Most Headteachers hadn't been teaching all day, they have been sat in their office planning the Agenda of torture for the workers. Nine agenda items to span ninety minutes, just what we all wanted!

However, just occasionally you need to have your wits about you or suddenly your name was down for something you would rather have avoided. During one particularly boring meeting where no one was really listening or joining in apart

Miss Ing RQT

from the Headteacher and the person whose curriculum area it happened to be that day, I suddenly found myself in the frame.

I think the discussion was about Information Technology. Looking around the room three staff were writing, one was doing her shopping list, the other his lottery ticket and a third an intricately shaded doodle. Two were looking out of the window, probably dreaming of holidays, two were staring at the floor playing spot the stain and thinking of who or what it resembled. Another three were 'in the zone' not sure where that was but not on planet Earth. Then came the fated moment, somewhere at the back of my head I heard the distorted sound of Miss Steak saying, "Sarah, I thought you would be the perfect person for that role?"

"Oh yes Miss Steak. Thank you."

"Wonderful," our Headteacher said, "so if there's no other business I will close the meeting."

Of course there were no other items to discuss, everyone just wanted to get out of the room. Gradually the place emptied with several staff nodding and smiling across to me in appreciation of what I had agreed to do. The two Year 5/6 teachers seemed to be smiling the most. But what exactly had I agreed to do? I thought I would go along to see Miss Steak and try to bluff my way to find out what it was. I knocked on the door and she beckoned me in. "Thank you so much for agreeing to take on that extra responsibility of being our Link Teacher."

Oh, the Link Teacher, I thought. Right then – link to what?

"What exactly does that involve Jos?" I enquired.

"Well Sarah it's really self-explanatory, isn't it my dear?" she said in a patronising tone.

"Yes I know," I continued to say, "but will it need a lot of my time? Who did it before me?"

"It was Mr Hart but after he crashed into the Head of Year 7's car last term, followed by the heated argument and giving him a black eye, it is probably best he did not continue with the role."

Year 7, I thought to myself silently. We don't have any Year 7 children. That is the start of secondary school. "And Miss Happ, what about her doing it? She has the other class with Y6 children in it?" I continued.

"Yes I know Sarah, but after her relationship with the secondary school vice principal finished it would prove very difficult for her as he usually attends all the primary/secondary meetings and runs the Year 6 parent information evenings when they visit our school. After you handled the dreadful situation with the twins last term and liaised with the agency staff for grief counselling and stress, I thought you were the stand out person for the extra responsibility. You will need some time out of the classroom for meetings with secondary staff and planning, but the bad news is…there's no extra money allowance with this, but it will look good with any future school for your C.V.," Miss Steak continued.

"But I might not want to be in a church school next," I replied naïvely.

"No silly, not C of E, C.V. Curriculum Vitae. You do make me laugh, Sarah."

Wow, so here I was half way through my second year of teaching and a promotion – even if there was no pay rise just yet. My name would be regularly up on the staff notice board showing me out attending meetings with the big school, extra time during the day for planning. I think I will look forward to this, so now I was Miss Sarah Ing – Link Teacher. Boris and I drove home proudly that evening, at our top speed of slow, but proud.

CHAPTER TEN
I HATE MONDAYS!

Most teachers hated Mondays, but the Monday all teachers hated was the one at the start of a week with a parents' consultation evening in it. Not because of meeting them but because you did a day and a half all in one day. If you escaped by 7:30pm you could count yourself lucky. In the spring term we had individual appointments with our parents over two evenings, usually Wednesday and Thursday. By the time staff stagger into school on the Friday they were exhausted before they actually started work. You can almost guarantee that the last parents in were ones that wanted more than the normal 10 minutes allowed and they knew that there would be no one waiting to see you after them. Our previous Headteacher, Mr Bush, used to rattle a big bunch of keys and even turned off the lights saying, "Sorry, I didn't think there could possibly be anyone still here, it being so late!" I really miss him.

I liked to talk with parents about their children and can often spot little habits or phrases that were common to both the parents and their child. Parents can sometimes be guilty of declaring too much information. I didn't really want to know what kind of birth their child had, their problems with toilet training, or exactly what they brought up when they were sick last week. A lot of parents wanted their child in a higher ability group for Maths or English, or given a harder reading book, but would then complain that their child was struggling and could I do more to help. A very small number would like their child in the next year group. Quite often a bright child could cope with this academically but not socially and it could do more harm than good in the long run.

Some parents asked their child every detail of the day at school and quoted it back to you like Chinese Whispers. You could guarantee that if you had any difficult parents to deal with you would bump into them the following week, probably in an unusual place like a music concert, the pub, public toilets or a festival rather than the local supermarket or street. On my final teaching practice as a student, the classroom teacher told me that schools would be wonderful places if it wasn't for the parents… and the children. On weeks like this one, I knew exact exactly what he meant.

My days of being a student teacher or even a newly qualified teacher seemed far away. You can't always turn to another member of staff straightaway for help and guidance, you received less praise and more paperwork was sent your way. College could often let students down when it came to the Foundation Subjects (Geography, History, Art, P.E., Music, CDT plus Child Protection) unless it happened to be their main subject.

One meeting I did look forward to was the occasional one when you met up with the other teachers in your area in the same year of teaching experience. It was great just to chat about each other's schools, with no Headteacher listening in of course. Some things were very similar but others were very,

very different. Swapping stories was always worthwhile. But most of the really funny ones came from the classes of the youngest children. Two of the teachers in our RQT group (Recently Qualified Teacher) taught the under-fives children, (known as Reception or Foundation in a primary or infant school). A parent told one of them that after the first day she asked her daughter how she had done today and the child replied, "Not enough, I've got to go back in again tomorrow."

The other teacher said that one of hers had been asked how he found school that day. He replied, "Well, I just jumped off the bus and there it was."

My contribution was telling the group about our recent parents' evening. One of them told me that their child thought he needed a new teacher. His Dad asked him why and he said, "She doesn't know anything, she keeps asking us for the answers."

This meeting took place in the spring term so memories of Christmas were still fresh in the minds of teachers, especially Key Stage One. A teacher with a class of Year 1 children had been doing Art with a group. They had done the nativity scene and the teacher could make out all the key figures and animals but was unsure about a shape at the back. On asking the child he said, "That's the stable bear Miss."

The final story came from a Year 2 teacher with a class of mainly six year olds. It was the final performance of the Nativity, but a lot of children were off school ill. A last minute Virgin Mary had to be found and she sat there dutifully showing her new born baby to everyone. However, she was obviously bored just sitting there, smiling and saying nothing.

So when the Wise Men turned up for the viewing she turned to them and said, "Isn't he lovely, he looks just like his Dad."

Over the next two months, Cliff and I went out several times for meals, a quiet drink or to the cinema. I even went to watch him play a few matches. By the end of the normal season they made it into the play-offs and won their home and away semi-final style games to reach Wembley. On one occasion my photograph appeared in the newspaper alongside Cliff and the camera even turned in my direction during the football match highlights on television after he scored. One of my friends referred to me as a WAG. This really confused me because I thought that was someone who told a lot of funny stories and that certainly was not a good description of me. But apparently it stands for 'Wives and Girlfriends' of professional footballers, so maybe that was me after all? Cliff had given up smoking and had only been booked once after that famous Friday night, Saturday morning when we first 'met'.

CHAPTER ELEVEN
RESIDENTIAL REVISITED

My second ever residential adventure with the Year 4s seemed to come around very quickly. Surely it was less than twelve months since that never ending series of back to back incidents. They now seemed really funny with hindsight, but at the time were adrenalin filled problems that needed solving instantly. A quick check of my diary confirmed that it was the same month, week and within a day of my first introduction to the never ending joys of transporting your class from an indoor to an outdoor classroom experience.

The first part of the trip was boring compared to last year's. All the children arrived on time, parents were organised, luggage and equipment loaded onto the coach without any bags bursting open, bottles leaking or medicines forgotten. All set and ready to go then – apart from Mr Hart! Mr P Hart the token male teacher required for all school trips these days. The man with the parents who were absent on the day they taught phonics at their school to help them with the sensible naming of their one and only son.

So there we all sat on the coach, fifty one children with four female adults, well three and a half anyway as one was

Miss Cheeseburger our new NQT, I thought to myself smugly. Our two trusty teaching assistants, Batman and Robin, were sitting ready once again, waiting for their first customer of the day to have their head in the sick bucket – fingers crossed we could make it more than five miles before those traffic light sweets started to work their magic, and praying that their first victim was not me. You remember them? The ones that make children's faces change colour and then they stick on green just before they throw up.

Mobile phones were being called into action to find the answer to the question of, 'Where is he?' Five minutes after our scheduled departure time, the muttering and Mumbling of the many parents gathered at the school gates to witness and truly verify that they would be without their children for a few days, now rose in volume to a worrying level. But over their drone was heard the noise of screeching tyres and a revving engine as the dirty outline of a once yellow Triumph Spitfire accelerated through the village ignoring the much stressed obedience of the speed limits close to school. Just as if a button had been pressed, a gap appeared through the middle of the throng of anxious parents big enough for the car to drive in and park inside the school gates. I say park but abandon would be a more accurate description as Mr Hart's car was left at a forty five degree angle across two parking lanes. A flustered male teacher flung open his car door with such ferocity that it bounced back and trapped the hand that had gripped the side of the car to help him haul his frame out of the low to the ground vehicle that was really far too sporty for his personality. A cry of pain as he slammed the door shut on his own hand was hidden by the sarcastic applause that spontaneously broke out from the impatient parents who had hoped to have waved goodbye to the coach load about ten minutes ago.

Mr Hart resembled a scarecrow with shirt hanging out, shoelaces flapping and an undone zip on the front of his trousers, but these were the least of his problems at this moment in time. He quickly grabbed his large bag and coat from the boot of the car, slammed the lid down and stumbled up the steps of the coach as the undone lace on his right shoe had the last laugh on the frazzled man. He threw his bag onto the only empty double seat remaining but before he could sit down the coach doors had closed, engine started and the coach driver took his revenge on the latecomer. The coach was underway with its customary jerk and jolt. It really wasn't Phil Hart's day as this movement took him completely by surprise. He missed grabbing the top of his seat's head rest, lurched over the back of it and landed face down on top of a surprised Mrs Poorly (TA). As an unshaven, unwashed, badly dressed and slightly smelly Mr Hart pushed himself off the shocked Teaching Assistant, the smile of satisfaction remained on her face for quite some time. He sat himself down at the second time of asking, reflecting on his manic start to the day, it then dawned on him the Triumph Spitfire car keys were not in his possession – they were still in the car ignition slot back at school.

Phil later explained to us that as he was going to be away for the week his wife had taken the opportunity to go and visit her mother. A decision he strongly supported as he didn't have to go with her on this occasion. However, it was usually his wife who was first up in the morning and in her absence, he had forgotten to set the alarm.

The still smiling Mrs Poorly subtly patrolled up and down the coach aisle on the lookout for any sick and needy to comfort. She always looked in on Mr Hart each time she passed him just in case he made a sudden movement in her direction and needed a welcoming cushion to break his fall. Having recovered from his mad dash, Phil only had one thing on his mind – to fall asleep. After all why would he be needed, he was only the most senior member of staff, organiser and teacher in charge. With the two teaching assistants, a newly qualified teacher and a recently qualified teacher, there surely couldn't possibly be a situation that they'd fail to cope with?

The coach stopped at about half way for an 'everybody make a single line and crocodile our way to the toilet' break. All 51 children trailed off whether they needed the toilets or not and four female adults carefully supervised them. Even the coach driver vacated his seat to seek refreshments, a comfort break and a possible boost to his chances of developing lung cancer. He checked behind him that all was clear, locked up the coach and set the alarms.

After a few minutes the teacher in charge of the residential trip opened one eye and an ear, puzzling why it was all quiet. Was he dreaming? Had he gone deaf? Were all the children sitting in absolute silence with their hands on top of their heads? Had all the children been captured by aliens and transported onto their spaceship, next stop galaxy 221B? No!

As he sat up and took in the new scenery outside the parked coach he realised that they were at a service area. He walked down to the front of the coach and tried the door that he had dashed through when doing his grand entrance of embarrassment back at the school gates. It was firmly locked. He twisted the driver's door but that too was very well secured. A feeling of being trapped started to creep over him as well as the need for a visit to the gents. Some of the children that he was in charge of appeared at a picnic table about 30 metres away. He knocked at the window as hard as he could and waved frantically. Phil was in luck, one of the St Alemate's children spotted him, nudged the others and they all waved back to him with smiling faces. Mr Hart's patience was now starting to wear thin. Well it matched his hairstyle anyway. In desperation for freedom and relief, our esteemed teacher in charge dashed to the back of the coach and pulled hard on the handle marked 'Emergency Exit'. The good news was that the door opened and the smell of fresh, cold, diesel, polluted air rushed onto the coach, but it was no match for the smell of 57 people all enclosed in a small area for well over an hour. But the bad news was that the previous silence had now been shattered by the deafening sound of the coach's horn, a World War II air raid siren and every possible light on the coach going on and off at a rapid pulse rate. Ooops!

The coach driver sprinted back towards his vehicle to challenge the thieves who must be trying to break into his charge. Phil Hart was half way out of the coach when the solid body weight of the out of breath driver collided with him taking them both to the damp, oily, diesel stained floor of the car park allotted for coaches and lorries. The pair rolled around for a few seconds in this catch weight wrestling bout until the driver emerged on top. He drew his clenched fist back its full distance only to be grabbed by all action TA Mrs Rucksack. At

Messy Coach Driver

that moment, all parties realised what the true situation was. The driver called the teacher in charge a few choice words that were better not heard by the Y4s even though most of the children had come across them before and too many had probably used them on one or two occasions.

The driver quickly dusted himself off, unlocked the coach and silenced the unwanted alarm. Mr Hart looked in horror at the wet marks and oil stains that now discoloured the clothes that were clean when he first put them on at 100mph with the clock showing 7.23am earlier this morning. I think it was the quickest I had ever seen fifty children clamber back onto a coach, find their seats and fasten up their seat belts. As the staff climbed aboard there was silence, I thought I heard some muffled, disguised sniggering when an oily Mr Hart came into view, but I can't be sure.

After only another fifteen minutes of the journey, James Little had a problem, he really needed the toilet. He didn't go when he had the chance at the service area because he didn't feel that he needed to – but he did regret that decision now! On one of her patrols, Mrs Poorly told him it would be about an hour until we reached the farm. A quarter of an hour later and James had passed the uncomfortable stage and was well into the desperately painful phase. He wasn't brave enough to ask for the toilet that was on the coach, especially since the bush telegraph at school had informed them all about the unfortunate incident of the Year 4 boy and the coach toilet on last year's trip!

James had a brainwave, it didn't happen very often so he thought he had better make the most of it. One of the reasons he needed to go to the toilet was because he had already emptied his quite large plastic drinks bottle. Therefore, he had a container with nothing in it sitting at the bottom of his bag and it had a tight lid to seal the top. He was sitting next to the window. He twisted himself around so that his body was facing the window with his back turned firmly on his best friend Alan Murfitt. James really hoped that Al would still be his best friend in about ten minutes time. No one took any notice of a boy opening the top of his drinks bottle and only one person on the coach knew what was going to happen next. Carefully placing the container between his knees and leaning slightly forward everything was now in place. All that remained was the release of all that unwanted liquid. It seemed to take a long time before the water escaped and found its new resting place. James delicately guided the stream and even found time to look over his shoulder at Alan, smile and look all casual, not an easy thing to do during this tricky operation. James found some satisfaction in this problem solving exercise with the watery stuff returning to its starting point from earlier in the day. All done he carefully put the lid on very, very, tightly, placed it back in the bottom of his rucksack and casually zipped up his jeans. He just hoped that Alan had lots of drink left and didn't ask him for any of his before they reached their destination.

The coach made really good time on the second part of the journey, anybody would think that the driver wanted rid of us. We were there so early that the previous school had not yet departed. They were from a northern county of England and two years older than our children. The driver just about managed to parallel-park alongside the other, soon to be departing, coach and the two sets of pupils and staff performed opposite images of each other's actions. The children from the other school seemed quite lively, large and loud compared to ours. Several of our children came to complain about them within minutes of us leaving the coach. One group said that a boy had called them a Norbert and wondered what it was. I searched out the boy in question and after asking one of his teachers to act as an interpreter discovered that he had said that he was, "No'but a dwarf", meaning he was very small. Another boy said that one of the Year 6s had threatened to hit him but he persuaded him against it in case the older boy hurt his hand during the action of thumping him. One day that boy will be a politician.

The other school seemed to be struggling to supervise their children and this was partly down to the fact that two of their adults just kept staring at each other. They only had eyes for one another and were clearly living on Planet Love and oblivious to the rest of the world. At last they were on their way home and following them down the track was our empty coach. Mr Hart did a quick head count and stopped at 52. The other four adults looked at him with a look that just said, 'You can't count'. Unfortunately, a female count also declared the number to be 52 and we suddenly realised that we had gained a Norbert. Mr Riddle, the farm owner quickly mobile phoned the other school and their coach returned for the northern lad. Everyone thought it was very funny apart from the two love struck teachers who hadn't even noticed the coach was back at the farm, they seemed to be having one of those staring competitions where you looked at each other until someone blinked.

Off the coach went again and we all picked up our bags and headed for the farm. James was in a really good mood now, not just because the damp patch on the front of his jeans had nearly dried but due to the fact that he had given his drinks bottle to one of the Year 6 children from the other school and waved it farewell…

CHAPTER TWELVE
DOWN ON THE FARM

I was told by those far more experienced than a RQT that no two residential visits were ever similar. In my limited experience, I can only agree fully with that statement. Mr and Mrs Riddle were still apologising for the events of last year and had given the school a 25% discount for being brave enough to return. We could look back and laugh at it now and Mrs Rucksack had got a new pair of boots out of it. The goats didn't look thrilled to see us back. Surely they couldn't remember us from 12 months ago could they? The speed at which they disappeared seemed to say that they did even if Mr Hart was in his oily disguise.

Just before Mr Hart went for a shower and a change of clothes he remarked to the farmer about a new mini-bus parked by the children's accommodation block (or cow shed as the cattle grazing in the next field called it). Mr Riddle explained that about six months ago another teacher had been caught out by seeing the ejected ignition keys on the floor while driving along, had panicked and collided with a tree that was minding its own business by the side of the road. Fortunately, there was no one else in the mini-bus at the time, the teacher was just shocked and shaken but the bus was a write off and had to be scrapped.

We all took our bags into our rooms, unpacked and started the settling in process. Some of the children thought that undoing the zips on their bags was enough to cover them for that requirement and quickly started their first game of, 'knock and run'. This involved exactly what it said on the tin, you chose a room to target, knocked loudly on it and legged it as quickly as you could. By the time one of the children opened the door and looked down the corridor there was either no one there or someone who hadn't a clue what you were talking about was blamed. Once or twice was just about acceptable, but when it reached double figures of knocking on the same door it could start to become tedious. The group of knockers took it in turns to do the deed but sometimes in the heat of the moment a feeling of nervousness before the rush of excitement could lead to panic and hitting the wrong door.

Poor Alan, he was having such fun with the other three boys that when it came to his turn again he was slightly inaccurate and rapped on the wrong door missing the frame target by one. Normally this wouldn't matter but on this occasion it meant he had pounded on Mr Hart's door. He wasn't in the room at that second but he was walking down the corridor heading back to his room after taking his much needed shower and washing away the majority of the oil slick that had become attached to him in the coach car park. Three of the boys had spotted Phil but Alan was concentrating too hard on completing his mission. He launched a vicious triple hit on the poor door, as he turned away from what he thought was a

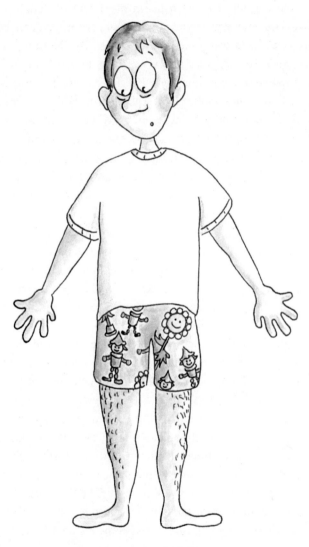

Mr Hart with Bill & Ben

successful task, Alan had a huge grin of delight on his face. His body was already on the run part of the game but the eyes and head were fixed on the target. By the time his head had turned 90 degrees and was facing forwards his progress was halted, the corridor went dark for a second or two and he ended up sitting on the floor. The other three boys had melted away by now and there were only two people in the corridor, Alan and Mr Hart. The teacher was in a clean t-shirt, bare feet and with a towel wrapped around his waist. The male teacher thought the drying material was wrapped tightly around his waist but he hadn't accounted for the impact of a little knock and runner head-butting him in the stomach, with a reflex action of grabbing onto anything as he bounced back. The next thing Alan remembered, was sitting on the floor with a damp towel in his hand, looking up at the images of Bill and Ben the Flower Pot Men and Little Weed. Mr Hart's favourite boxer shorts were now exposed for anyone to see, and they did. It was as if someone had pressed a button and all the doors up and down the corridor opened and heads poked out at all heights to stare at this unusual sight. An embarrassed Mr Hart grabbed back his towel and fled to the sanctuary of his room. The secret of what children's TV programmes had been his favourite was now known to all of Year 4 and by the end of next week probably the whole school, even if they had never heard of these three strangely uncoordinated characters urgently in need of speech therapy. Alan's status had been raised to hero in just a few seconds and he thoroughly enjoyed his fifteen minutes of fame. He was also extremely glad not to be in Mr Hart's group for the rest of the residential week.

Looking through all the forms that had been returned by parents was quite entertaining. I don't just mean the variation on spellings but, for example, in the parent employment section one had put 'Income Sport'. The number of different allergies and serious reactions by children to various things was amazing these days. There were the usual suspects of nuts, dairy products, eggs, gluten free and shell fish but we also had a child who reacted to the smell of fresh paint. Apparently, she could pass out if it was strong and may need 'rhesus' according to her parents' form. There was an amazing number of sleep walkers according to the information sheets, I had this vision of them all being on the move at the same time. It would look like a scene from a 'Waking the Walking Dead' horror film – spooky! In addition, there were quite a few bed wetters and I resolved to make sure none of them were sleeping on a top bunk when I did my checks later on.

About 3.30am I was woken up by a loud noise from the children's room next door to me. This came as quite a shock as I didn't realise that the time 3.30 happened twice in one day. I lay there for a few minutes wondering what the noise could have been and listened for any similar repeats. It all went quiet but I thought I'd better go and check, hoping the zombies were all safely tucked up in their beds. Quietly, I opened their door but it always amazed me how noisy doors were in the middle of the night, I think they saved up all their creaks and squeaks just to have a bigger effect and be noticed. The light from the corridor streamed in to show a pile of clothes in the middle of the floor. Nothing unusual about that I thought especially as it was an all boys' room. Everything seemed okay but just as I had started to close the door the pile moved and groaned. Yes, it was a pile of clothes but someone was wearing them. The mixture of pyjamas, dressing gown, socks, slippers and a sleeping bag were being modelled tonight by Ashley. He had started off on the top bunk but now he was back at floor level. Had he knocked himself out? Was he injured? I quickly knelt down beside him doing my Florence Nightingale impersonation and whispered, "Are you awake Ashley?"

"No!" was the firm reply and the pile of jumble turned over and started to snore. I couldn't just leave him on the floor, could I? But if I put him back and he fell off again he might not bounce this time and could really hurt himself. Ashley looked fine there on the floor, and safe, so I decided to leave him for a few more hours. Later I could swap him with a lower bunker who wasn't a bed wetter or one of the walking dead gang. "Night Mum," came the words from the talking clothes pile as I slowly closed the room door.

The next morning I called in to see if Ashley was fit and well. He didn't remember a thing and was really embarrassed that he had called me, 'Mum'. We made sure all the children showered before breakfast on that first morning, though some were rather reluctant. Elizabeth looked at us with disgust at the idea and argued, "What! You mean with soap?"

Cooked breakfasts on a residential trip were always worth looking forward to but not as good as I remembered when I was at primary school and we had to cook our own. They provided all the ingredients and we took it in turns to prepare it with one of the teachers. Cooking scrambled eggs for forty was great fun. Sadly, the ogres of the Health and Safety Department had now put a stop to all that memory filled fun.

We did a few different things to last year. I think Mr P Hart was making his mark being the organiser, having taken over from Mrs (Chlora) Form. One new visit was to a local museum where they had a special exhibition about the

Romans. Kate became very excited at the sight of a Roman soldier walking around the place and remarked several times that we were, "So lucky to have a real live Roman to help us with our project work."

Bless her!

Just before we left the museum to set off back to the farm we did the ritual of stopping off at the toilets. Being a museum they were for any visitors and there seemed to be a group of senior citizens slowly touring around the place. Our token male went in with the boys who needed to go, plus several who didn't (they just liked to visit all the rooms in the place). Maria went in with the girls and I waited outside with the others. Well, I waited outside until I heard a high pitched scream of pain from inside the ladies section of the toilets. Suzanne was the owner of the scream, it was certainly justified as her fingers were trapped in one of the cubicle doors and it was firmly shut and locked. She was just standing outside the cubicle door talking to one of her friends with her hand holding onto the frame, not realising that part of the door was next to the hinge. Miss Cheeseburger and Mrs Poorly were hammering on the door but the senior citizen occupying the small room was not responding – perhaps it was a hearing aid malfunction? I did something that I hadn't been guilty of since being at my secondary school. I stood on the closed toilet seat next door and looked over the side. A little old lady was sitting there looking like she had nodded off. I think it was my waving arms as well as the shouting that caught her attention and after first thinking she was hearing voices from on high she told me to buzz off but then realised something was wrong, pulled herself together and opened the toilet door. By this time, Suzanne had gone very pale and was close to fainting. Batman and Robin, our two crusty (sorry, trusty) TAs cast their First Aid trained eyes over the injury and both agreed she … needed a second opinion and a trip to the local hospital.

Three hours later Suzanne and I were still in Accident and Emergency awaiting the results of an X-ray. All the others had gone back to the farm and someone would come back for us when I telephoned for a lift. We had missed tea hours ago and the funny people who couldn't walk properly, had been sick over themselves, were shouting at everyone, but needed subtitles and were injured, had started to arrive at A&E. It was really quite scary. Someone should film these people and then replay it to them the next morning.

A very, very nice looking young doctor arrived to give us the verdict. I think he must have been about my age and height. His voice was soft but authoritative and his eyes almost magnetising. Dr Hunk had blue eyes and was wearing my favourite aftershave for men (well it was now). Apparently, he said that Suzanne had no broken fingers just badly bruised ones and that she had been lucky. I rang Mr Hart and he came to tear us away from the hospital and my new found friend in a smart, whiter than white, beautifully fitted coat. They had saved us some food, though Suzanne ate very little that evening so I helped her out on this occasion. Our wonderful Year 4 girl survived thanks to the boost of sympathy received from the majority of the girls.

Our leader Phil shocked us by suggesting that the four female adults took a drive into the village for a drink at the local pub and a change of scenery after the children had settled down. Wow! The children were tucked up in bed in record time that evening, whether they wanted to or not. Within one hour of our leader's kind offer we were heading for the village hostelry, 'The Singing Ferret'. It was a quaint looking pub and we were greeted by the local custom, of such places, by everyone in the place. All the regulars huddled round the bar turned to stare at us and all conversation stopped. As we stood at the bar smiling sweetly at the welcoming scowl from the landlord, his opening words of greeting were: "You lost then? Broken down? Eh?"

We noticed that the pub's Alsatian dog was loose behind the bar and licking the nozzles where the beer poured down into the glass. So bottled beer it was then, apart from Mrs Rucksack who was this evening's Des (designated driver). The landlord's name was Guy. He didn't volunteer this. It was on a large sign behind the bar, 'Guy gives you a warm welcome to his friendly village pub' – liar! I expect he's only popular around November 5th.

One or two of the locals started their mutterings again, in between casting glares and glances in our direction. The pool table was free so why not, anything to liven this place up. Maria had just bent down to push in the £1 coin to release the balls when she came face to face with the pub rabbit. It was a cute, white, little creature that apparently lived inside the workings of the pool table. Judging by the small round deposits spread around the green baize, he only usually popped up to the surface when he felt the urge, or someone was threatening his 'burrow'. We sat down in the corner, slowly drank up, said very little, returned the hostile glances, then we went back to the farm.

The last few days went well with our only other problem happening on the final morning. Peter had a real worry with his feet. They had both enlarged so much he couldn't put his shoes on. I checked just in case he had the wrong pair but his

103

name had been clearly written inside both. It didn't matter how loose I made the laces his feet would not slide into the shoes. Reluctantly, as a last resort, I decided his socks would have to be removed. This took a while as after I removed a blue pair I was faced with a red pair, followed by a green one, then yellow and a pair that I think were probably once white. Apparently, his Mum had repeatedly stressed to him that he had to put a clean pair on every day. Dutifully, Peter had done exactly that but without taking any off – his Mum had said nothing about removing the pair worn the day before.

We set off for home on the same coach that had brought us but not the same driver, he had phoned in sick that morning. Mr and Mrs Riddle, the goats and various other animals all came to see us off and we quickly settled down to falling asleep for the return journey. Thankfully, it was Friday so I could have a lie in tomorrow morning. Then take Alfie for a long walk after his week long holiday staying with Molly, a friend of mine from the football team. We had a big game on Sunday morning, cup semi-final against Hornville Hornets. I wondered if Cliff had missed me.

Cliff was actually waiting for me when I arrived home, eventually, from my week away on the school residential visit. He was loaded up with a takeaway meal that had gone cold, but that was probably my fault as I hadn't gone straight home to what I thought was an empty flat. We talked for hours after the meal and I actually fell asleep half way through a sentence, so when I woke up hours later he had gone home and I was still on the settee.

CHAPTER THIRTEEN
HYDE THE JEKYLL

Something really strange happened to children outside of the school environment. Many changed into a completely different child, an unrecognisable monster from the one that teachers saw five days a week and 38 weeks of the year. The little boy or girl who, if allowed, would quietly sit at the back of the classroom, rarely put up a hand or contribute to discussions but when out with parents suddenly had an attack of that nasty illness – the 'verbal diarrhoea'. It was an uncontrollable disease that could last for two days over the weekend and then just disappeared around 9am on a Monday morning.

Sometimes it could be the reserved, drowsy styled, blonde haired girl who transformed after 3.30pm into the child who sat screaming on the floor of the local supermarket or removed the pivotal tin from the tall stack of vegetables on display at the end of the aisle.

Even on the sports field, the child who represented their school with perfect fair play and genuine respect for the opposition metamorphosed into a snarling, spitting, foul mouthed little hooligan playing sport at weekends.

At meal times, the angelic, well-mannered child sat amongst his or her peers quite happily on a Monday to Friday lunchtime but was different again when taken to a restaurant or up market café with parents or grandparents and the altered character was quite shocking. Suddenly they were incapable of placing their bottom on a chair for more than 10 seconds. They shouted, screamed, waved their arms about, sulked and stamped their feet – all of this before the food had arrived.

Trains, boats and planes don't really need to supply seats for many children. They should seriously think about producing a caged off, sound proofed ball pool in a bouncy castle styled corner, just next to the emergency escape door with a built in strong fabric slide.

Hundreds of children throughout the land aged from 4 to 11 can sit in special Assemblies, plays, shows or demonstrations for over an hour without anyone needing to be fed, watered, go to the toilet or even speak. But take them to a big sporting event as a spectator or a play, film or show that the adult particularly wanted to see, and thought the child would enjoy it as well, and the transformation stage once again kicked in. As soon as you have made your way past half the people sat in your row (on such occasions your seats were always in the middle) the child needed to visit the loo or felt hungry or thirsty. But rest assured these needs never occurred at the same time but would be interspersed with gaps of about 2 to 5 minutes from asking all those people, unknown to you, to stand up so you can make your way to and from your booked seat. It was also almost guaranteed that while you were away from the action someone had scored or you would have missed the crucial part of the performance.

Living not far from school, I often met children and their parents in places like the local supermarket. Some children don't actually think that a teacher can exist outside the walls of their classroom and school. So it can be quite a shock to meet up with them in the frozen food aisle. Some children stood and stared with shock, horror and amazement. Others smiled sweetly and said, 'Hello Miss'. But a third group can act very strangely, their normal character changed dramatically. These were the ones who started to behave. This change came as quite a shock to their parents. One minute they had a whining, annoying little child begging for sweets and putting things in the trolley that they were not allowed. But in the next instance the child was quietly stood by the trolley and moved on at the same time as the week's supply of food and in the proper direction.

This happened to me again last week when I met Laura from my class with her Mum and baby brother. As I turned into the sweets and biscuits section there was Laura sitting in the middle of the floor, arms firmly folded and a look of evil spread across her face. The moment we made eye contact she jumped up, ran over to her mother's side and held on to the metal trolley. "Now what Laura?" Mum shouted. "What's wrong with you? Why are you doing as you are told? What have you done this time?"

I decided to give that aisle a miss for now and headed towards the washing powder. There shouldn't be too many little dears down that part of the store.

CHAPTER FOURTEEN

SUPPLY AND DEMAND

Meetings between primary and secondary staff increased as we went through the academic year and my role of Link Teacher was gradually becoming clearer. These meetings often meant that my class would be covered by a supply teacher. Whenever the class realised this their mood changed. The class that was always well behaved, attentive and quiet became restless, chatty and disruptive. A different class that was a handful for their normal teacher was a nightmare and bordered on riotous in the care of a stranger. In some ways being on supply was a great way to teach. You visited many schools, different aged classes and met a lot of teachers. There was usually very little marking especially if you could manage to exit quickly before anyone realised you had 'forgotten' to complete all the work the children should have done. Your rate of pay was higher than most teachers because your salary was calculated by dividing the number of teaching days (usually 190) into a teacher's annual wage. There were no parent/teacher discussions to attend or reports to write or staff meetings to be bored by.

But on the downside, you hardly ever had your own class group of children for very long. No holiday pay. You usually ended up doing a lot of playground duties, as it always seemed to be the turn of the teacher you were booked to cover whether they were on a course, at a meeting, doctor's appointment, a funeral or just ill. Every school was slightly different on discipline, marking, moving around, group work or even going to the toilet! Some teachers left pages of notes, details, instructions, suggestions or options – others nothing.

Discipline was probably the most difficult part of the daily routine. You could easily find yourself teaching Reception before break (under 5s) and Y6 after break (11 year olds). A friend of mine couldn't find a full time job straight away so went on the supply list for the secondary school age range even though he was still officially a NQT. During his first time at an inner city secondary school he had to take a Y7 class for P.E. Unfortunately, part of this included supervision in the boys changing rooms. On their way through to the gym area, the group getting changed from the lesson before were Y10s (15 year olds). They instantly recognised a new, young teacher in their midst and began to be very cheeky to my friend. This included swearing and various suggestions about his pony tail.

After several reminders about their behaviour and empty threats regarding possible punishment, he lost his cool. He approached the ring leader, just managed to grab hold of his front enough to lift him off his feet and hung him on the nearest peg by the back of his jacket collar. His legs were kicking wildly, but just above the floor, and his arms were flapping away like a new born baby bird. The Y7s thought it was hilarious. The other Y10s quickly picked up their kit bags and fled. My friend thought he would leave naughty Nigel, the

Y10, for a few minutes while he organised the start of his lesson for the Y7 group. This was a big mistake. Unfortunately for him the secondary school Principal (Headteacher) had seen the fleeing of 14 Y10 boys sprinting down the corridor. He had not said a word to them but entered the boys changing room to discover a quietly simpering Y10 Nigel, (so called hard man) hanging all alone on the peg. "What exactly do you think you are doing Normanton?" barked the Principal, feeling braver on finding only one pupil there!

"Sir, sir, it was that new long haired teacher. He assaulted me and left me hanging here."

The Principal peeked into the gym to find out who this new teacher was, then turned and walked straight past naughty Nigel Normanton with the passing words, "You just stay there boy, don't go anywhere."

The Principal headed directly for the Head of P.E. to enquire about the Y10 hanging by Mr Pony Tail. He, of course was totally baffled but as it was a query from his boss he thought he had better investigate. He released Nigel from captivity, knowing that he was probably the cause of the problem. But my friend was never asked back to teach there again.

I also remember one occasion when I had to attend a two day course and leave my class in the charge of a new supply teacher. On my return she thanked me for all the notes I had left but wrote that she had experienced a few problems with Millie (in English) and Glen (during History). This baffled me as they were two of the quietest children in the class and never

Miss Ing

in any trouble. Later in the morning when I had a quieter moment I deliberately asked Millie to come out and read to me. After asking her about the two days with Mrs Longbottom, (the supply teacher) she eventually told me about the difference of opinion during Wednesday's literacy hour. "She asked me to say a sentence with the word 'I' in it but every time I started she kept interrupting me, Miss."

"Oh," I replied, "why did she keep interrupting you?"

"Well," continued Millie, "I kept starting my sentence with, 'I is' and she stopped me every time saying it had to be I am."

I nodded sympathetically and she further explained, "So when I said oh all right then if you insist and said, 'I am the ninth letter of the alphabet', she went all huffy on me and told me to sit down."

That was one puzzle solved so what about Glen, he just happened to be next on my hit list for reading. He told me that they heard the story of the first President of the USA, George Washington, when he was a little boy. One day young George was walking around their garden with an axe, (as you do) and he chopped down his father's favourite tree. On finding this out his father was furious and asked everyone if they knew anything about it.

"Mrs Longbottom then asked us why his Dad didn't punish him for chopping it down after George admitted that it was him. I put my hand up and answered that it was because he still had the axe in his hand at the time and she said I was being 'flip and ant' or something like that and told me to keep quiet."

"I see," I replied, trying desperately to keep a straight face, "I can understand your answer Glen but she doesn't know you as well as I do and perhaps thought you were trying to be funny, but I thought it was a perceptive answer."

Glen looked rather insulted by my words and said, "I don't use a purse Miss, that's for girls. I have a wallet."

At that, I thought it was best to smile sweetly and end the conversation.

CHAPTER FIFTEEN

THE LINKER

My new found role of unpaid responsibility didn't really kick in until the start of the summer term. By then, thoughts turned to Key Stage Two records with teachers estimating SAT scores from the secondary point of view and keeping the Year 6s focused, at least until the half term. There were mini projects aimed at primary/secondary transfer and several familiarisation meetings. Each child had a lot of assessments, reports and test results that covered the foundation stage of their education and Key Stage One up to the age of seven, but little was wanted by the secondary school for that period, unless there was a problem.

All the other primary teachers from the various feeder schools had classes of just Year 6 or Year 5 and 6 children, except for one... me of course. The secondary teachers all seemed surprised at this fact until they learned the name of my school. This was then followed by one of those knowing looks that needed no words, just an assumption that they knew the real circumstances why. Most of the secondary teachers seemed very pleasant but a few had the manner and body language that suggested they were above me. It was as if the fact that they taught an older age group meant that they were more important, better qualified and overall superior to a mere teacher from Key Stage 2.

Once again the subject of teachers' names raised its humorous head with some of my secondary peers. There were about 10 or 11 of them attending the meeting, each one taking charge of a group for things like registration, PSHE and sorting out any problems a child might have at school. Archie Meedees was a Maths teacher, Miss Reid was from the English department, Madam Demure was French, of course, together with her future successor Clair Voyant and Miss T Morning, Science.

At age 11 transfer from primary to secondary education, or Key Stage 2 to Key Stage 3, can be a difficult one for many children and older brothers or sisters can sometimes make things worse by making up or exaggerating stories that may or may not have happened to them. Our old friends the school toilets will often be mentioned along with such words as 'head', 'toilet' and 'down'. Talking to children at the secondary school who attended St Alemate's a year ago was an interesting experience. A number of them recollected stories of being told strange things by secondary teachers early on in their first year there, year seven. For example:

"Your education starts now."

"You can't speak French unless taught it by a proper French speaking person."

"There's only one way to do Maths and that's my way."

Fortunately, the vast majority of secondary teachers were sensible, understanding and nearly normal. A few had even

115

.

ventured into primary classrooms to observe the wonders of the Literacy and Numeracy hours. Virtually all teachers of secondary subjects felt that not enough time was given to their particular subject in primary schools and even if their subject was given sufficient time, few agreed that it was taught properly. I don't think I could ever teach at a secondary school, well not successfully anyway. Something strange happened to a lot of children during their 'change'. That six week period over the summer holidays when they go from being reasonably normal and changed into something less human more stroppy and unsympathetic – what caused that? On occasions, secondary school staff contacted primary schools to ask if they had sent the correct report with certain children as their description no longer matched the strange creatures that had just walked into their school.

Some secondary schools had completely different opportunities for children from Year 7 onwards and that was great (I think). At our senior school they had a noticeboard where children could put adverts up to sell things. However, on the day I stopped to read it, I wondered how long ago it was since anyone had bothered to scan it with a view to possible censorship. One pink card read, 'FOR SALE – parachute, only used once, never opened, has a small stain'. Another said, 'Energizer Bunny arrested! Charged with battery'. Plus, 'Friction is a real drag!' Down one side it read, 'I bet you I could give up gambling', and 'Everyone has a photographic memory but some just don't have any film!'

Smiling, I walked on my way.

Assemblies seemed to be quite different from each other in the primary and secondary schools. Most of the younger children experienced one every day, but the older pupils might

116

only have it once a week during some times of the academic year. Primaries can experience such a wide variety of daily assemblies from their Headteacher/Deputy Head/Senior teacher, to visiting Church groups, the Fuzzy Felt man telling Bible stories, drama groups with really funny stories that the children love and have a vague reference to the Bible or Jesus thrown in for good luck near the end. Then there is the local vicar who doesn't say prayers, other Church representatives who just don't want to be there and hate every minute, or those who wind up the children so much that by the time they returned to their classrooms they were bouncing off the walls. Some clergy have the knack of sending their audience into sleep mode. It must be all that sermon practice on Sundays. Other visitors with all their goodwill seemed to adopt the Sunday School teacher approach. This can work with children below the age of nine but the older ones can take advantage and cause the teachers on duty quite a headache.

Annual festivals like Harvest used to be a key part of the autumn term in primary schools, with vast collections boxed up and taken around the community to the elderly and the needy. But nowadays staff would need danger money if they were brave enough to knock on a door with free food. Very few take it and even fewer were grateful, so schools could often be left with a pile of unwanted produce unless they happen to have an old people's home nearby. It always amused me to find the rosy red apple in the middle of the donations with a bite taken out to leave that brown stain mark in the once whole fruit.

Class Assemblies were always good value at primary schools, the younger a group the more entertaining they tended to be, especially when they were trying to be very serious.

Class groups normally did at least one a year to show off some of their work to parents and grandparents, as well as to the rest of the school. Singing can be great fun, especially when the music is coming from one end of the room in a large hall. There often seemed to be a slight time delay which created a Mexican Wave style effect of the words. It even sounded like they were singing a musical round when one half raced ahead of the other and they each ended at different times. Experiments were often shown during class assemblies and if they were not placed high enough to start with, it could cause that ripple effect across the room as children stretched, knelt, crouched and even stood higher to gain a better view. The ones who needed to watch closest of all were the little people on the front row, fidgeting quietly (sometimes), just minding their own business. Usually, when they glanced away was the moment that part of the science show, often liquid, hit them on the head or in the face. The younger children of the shy and quiet group were the ones that could shock everyone, especially their parents, by appearing to have swallowed a megaphone and caused the front four rows to sway back. However, the noisiest child in the class, on such occasions, could often impersonate someone miming or appeared to have suddenly acquired laryngitis.

CHAPTER SIXTEEN

TOILET TIME - HANDS UP!!!

There was something special and unique about school toilets. By the time Year 6s were thinking back on their years at primary school, most of them would have a memory or a tale or two to tell about something that happened on that hallowed ground.

Children in Reception, and even Year 1, seemed to spend a vast amount of their time going to, from, or in the toilets especially at the start of the school year in September. The range of the toilet pan size was an interesting one to ponder. At Nursery, Pre-school or Reception, the children often had toilets to suit the size of the little people that occupied that particular age range. As they progressed through the school the pan, cubicle and standing toilet area would change accordingly through Key Stages 1 and 2, but nowhere else in life did this happen. There might occasionally be a lower level standing area inside for males, so they tell me, but not for anyone else. Not at home, not in public conveniences, not in hotels! So why do schools spend billions of pounds to install small toilets throughout the land. Was this the idea of an over-priced plumber? Or the Department for Education? Or Ofsted? Please don't say Health and Safety again, or Elf and Slavery as a child once said to me.

Were children's toilets haunted? Many think so. Thousands of children will try not to go into the school toilets because of strange stories that had been put in their minds. There will often be rumours that someone heard rattling noises that sounded just like chains or strange voices called out during the quiet of the day. Toilets could be lonely places for our youngsters. Is it any wonder that so many had their, 'accidents' at school and phone calls then made by Nursery Nurses and Teaching Assistants for that clean change of clothing? How many times had a parent arrived at school following such a request with the words, "Well, it doesn't happen at home."

Bullying and teasing can happen in just about every primary school. Simply naïve is the Headteacher who foolishly says, "There's no bullying in this school, I would know about it."

The ones who lived in the real world were the Heads who knew it happened but realised that finding out about it was the hard problem to solve.

The toilet area could be an easy target place for the school bully – every year group in every establishment had one or more of them and most of the children could easily name him, or occasionally her, if asked. Any school in the land worth its salt will know this and have strategies in place to combat it – always worth an ask on new parents' information evenings.

Haunted toilets, especially the girls, was a thing of legend in school folk lore. Yes, these buildings had a lot of ventilation holes, often in roof lights. Yes, such areas could catch the wind and rattle, whistle and creak away merrily. If you are a child in there alone, especially sitting, it could be a strange and eerie experience. Were school toilets haunted? In reality no, but in the mind of an impressionable child – you better believe it!

For many the school toilet experience can be the encounter of a lifetime, a thing that could remain with them for ever, for either a good, bad or funny reason. In primary schools, younger children might have to use the main toilets for part of the day due to organisational or practical reasons. These times could have a significant bearing, for a young child, on the rest of their lives. The experience of sitting on the toilet seat in a strange land, behind a closed, locked, door surrounded by steep barricades, listening to the sounds of the main door open, can be horrific. Footsteps can be heard loud, heavy and echoing around the room. They stopped on the other side of your cubicle door, you sat waiting to see if a head appeared above the partition to look down on your privacy or a leering face appeared under the door you locked moments ago. Sometimes if the footsteps paused outside your cubicle door you soon discovered that a future, world famous safe cracker or escapologist had discovered the code to opening your toilet door from the outside. Was it any wonder that so many children had memories based in school toilets when they recalled their recollections of school?

The gender difference can often be quite wide ranging, with boys experiencing mild bullying from a gentle push forward at an off balance moment while standing there

Girls in Toilet

relieving themselves, to a trouser wetting threat from the school bully or another who saw himself as the likely successor in the years ahead. But for girls it can often be just an extension place of the school playground, a time to chat and laugh with others from different classes as well as their own. Or older, less confident girls see it as a chance to impress younger girls with stories of bravery and grown up ideas with the occasional naughty word thrown in for good effect. Often when checked by adults they find that there could even be several girls inside one cubicle like a social gathering in the old public phone box of years ago – eight is the record number that I had found in one cubicle so far. It was always annoying how the social numbers gathering increased in certain age groups during the introduction of the curriculum dealing with the, 'My Body' and 'Sex Education' sections of Personal, Social and Health Education. It was a crucial area of school behaviour and activity but how many of our schools had a policy or guidelines that covered the safe sanctuary of their school toilets? My guess was very few.

Louise Over was a lovely girl, nine years old, really kind to everyone and with a wonderful smile. Unfortunately, the minuses far outweighed the positives for poor Louise. Children can be so cruel to each other and will often pick on the slightest fault or weakness of another child. Louise didn't have any slight faults, no all of hers were huge.

Children and adults often have the habit of trying to shorten your name, however long or short it was to start with. Louise was called all sorts of names from Louse, Loose, Loser, Easy, Wheeze and many more. Lou was one of the most common. Now one of her many problems was in the bladder department and she had to visit the toilets on numerous occasions during the school day. She even had special permission from the teacher so she didn't have to ask to go, she could just leave the room whenever she needed to. Over the years her many nicknames developed into one main name now, 'Loulou'. She had learned to live with it and usually answered to it instinctively.

Anyone having a conversation with Louise always felt a little uncomfortable. People didn't know where to look. Sadly, Louise had a problem with her eyes as they seemed to move and look in opposite directions to each other. To try and correct this she usually wore glasses but the three pairs supplied by her parents were not always enough to provide her with an unbroken pair to wear every day of the five day school week. Her school work was not great and she was in the lowest group for most things. This group was called the leopards (at the moment), or as the other three groups cruelly named it – the Lepers.

The little people (children aged 4 and 5) seemed to spend about half of their academic lives either visiting the toilet, being told to go or being told how to tell an adult that they wanted to, might want to, needed to or were just thinking about going. This then created and led onto many breaks in a little person's important time of learning. Often at the vital stage of key questioning during a potentially life changing moment of learning, a hand went up just at the right time in the lesson. In school Assembly the teacher could discover that it was not THE vital answer he or she was seeking but a request to leave the room. On departing, that individual learner would probably never hear the vital answer to the subject in question because it was unlikely that they would be, 'filled in' on their return. This could create a gap in his or her learning that might affect them for the rest of their life. Toilets certainly had a lot to answer for in a small person's life.

It was interesting to note that at this early age the need will arrive about every thirty minutes to visit that place of unusual smells, that place of a different temperature to anywhere else in the school and the place where doors seem to creak and squeak more than any other doors in the entire building. A whole school Assembly can last around 15 or 20 minutes and you can guarantee that some of the little people will need to leave the room even if their teacher, nursery nurse, teaching assistant and volunteer parent helper had made sure that they all entered the creaky, cold, smelly room on the way to the Hall. In addition, when all the little bottoms have stood up and walked out of the Hall at the end of the whole school gathering, there would be a new mini lake that had appeared on the floor or a yellow stream slowly, smoothly, sliding its way across the polished floor.

However, miracles can occur amongst the little people. If there happened to be a particular interesting visiting speaker, or a film to be shown, or a play to be watched and it lasts for an hour plus, no new lakes or streams spring up through the hall flooring! Often there are no requests to leave the room and no one has fallen asleep (usually). This strange phenomenon is not only true of the youngest children. Even the oldest ones can last for hours on end if the lesson content is interesting. There is no need for them to feel the urge to stretch their legs, walk around school, have a pre-arranged chat with someone from another class or just to have a nose in someone else's bag. A large percentage of our lives can be spent being in, thinking about, walking to and from, avoiding and queuing for toilets. So why can't we make them more hygienic, less smelly and decrease the chances of it being a threat to our health?

CHAPTER SEVENTEEN
CHARACTER CHORUS

Most schools had their staff characters outside of the teaching group and at St Alemate's we had Alf, or as the children called him, 'Elf'. He was the extra person who only worked very part-time at all sorts of things around the school. It could be the gardens, fields, playgrounds, cutting back trees, bushes or hedges. But, no matter what task he was set, one thing was guaranteed and that was it would go wrong. Alf was the kindest guy you could ever wish to meet, but he was just jinxed. At one of his previous jobs in a factory, he was nicknamed Jonah. It wasn't his fault, I suppose, but anything that could go wrong, anything that could break, anything that could be lost or used the wrong way and made a mess of, just did.

One day he was trimming back the bushes that grew up against the office wall using his electric hedge cutter. Later that afternoon, Mrs Ored (school secretary) tried to phone out, but found that the line was dead. In the end she had to use her mobile phone to report the fault and the engineer came out the following day. It baffled him for a while until he started to

Alf the Annihilator

follow the line from the offices, through the wall to the outside where it disappeared through the bushes up to the edge of the roof and along to the telegraph pole.

Gently pushing his way through the foliage he found the telephone wire, in fact, he found four. A few years ago it was one but it had now multiplied thanks to Alf's hedge trimmer. Two of the broken ends had some sort of dirty sellotape wrapped around them in a bodged attempt to re-join the breaks. Alf denied all knowledge of the damage and casually blamed it on the local wildlife but he had left his calling card all over it.

One Sunday lunchtime I went to the local pub for lunch with my parents and saw our Alf at the other side of the room. He was with a group of people and carrying a tray full of about six drinks back to their table. He placed the tray half on and half off the table and casually picked up the 2 pint glasses that were on the side overlapping onto the table. To his utter astonishment the other four drinks then somersaulted through the air and crashed onto the floor, emptying their contents all over his shoes and socks. All of his group burst out laughing and the rest of the people in the pub turned to stare at the cause of the hilarity and noise. Poor Alf! What a loser.

On another occasion Alf was trimming back some overgrown hedges with the hand shears. Later he complained to the caretaker about how tough some of the work had been. What he failed to realise was that he had massacred the school's TV aerial cable and that it now resembled spaghetti. He was obviously not learning through his previous experiences and a third disaster soon awaited him after he used the secateurs to trim back the roses and sabotaged the school burglar alarm. The police car roaring into school with its siren blaring and headlights flashing looked really impressive as it skidded to a halt, but they were less than happy to discover it was a false alarm. Apparently, the alarm was triggered if the line was cut at any time.

Later in the year, he completed his full set by slicing through the computer Internet and Network line with a Stanley knife. No one bothered to ask what he was doing at the time. They just decided to let him go and gave him a month's notice before terminating his contract. A shame really, but I don't think the school could afford to employ him here anymore. He was just too expensive to keep on. I was sure he would find another job but for how long was another question.

Another character at St Alemate's was Mrs Bunter. She didn't mean to be, or try to be, a character, it just seemed to happen naturally. To say that she was larger-than-life would be a gross understatement. Beryl had taught at the school for about 10 years and some of the more cynical members of staff thought that was also the number that her dress size had increased by since the start of her teaching career there. She was a quiet, private person but I liked her. She had been kind to me when I started at the school and was always more than happy to help me if she possibly could.

Some aspects of being a Headteacher came naturally to Miss Steak and delegation was certainly at, or near, the top of that list. The staff meeting when she volunteered poor Beryl into being our Healthy Lifestyle Coordinator was one that will live long in my memory. Ms Steak (as she now preferred) complimented Mrs Bunter beautifully on her ability to possibly lead a curriculum area and the quality leadership skills Beryl apparently possessed. Most of the staff were expecting a core subject to be announced such as Maths or Science. So when

Health and Fitness eventually came out of her mouth it was quite a surprise. It was really funny, almost cruel, but nobody dare laugh, snigger or even smirk slightly in case Jos changed her mind and awarded the title to them for showing their happiness.

Beryl Bunter shuffled about uncomfortably on her seat. She went slightly red with embarrassment and glanced around the room. No staff eyes met hers apart from the Head. Those very senior management eyes were focused intently on her victim and she hovered menacingly like a hawk above her prey, before finishing off with the deadly swoop. Poor BB knew struggling was futile and looked around for her stress relief lever…food! There were four biscuits left in the staff tin, the usual suspects, biscuits that were always the last ones to be devoured, no chocolate or sweet coating anywhere, very plain, very boring and completely tasteless. There was also a thin slice of someone's birthday cake that had been waiting around for about a week. They would have to do in this emergency situation. Without hesitation, she used the tin lid as a plate and made the biscuits and cake evaporate completely, not a crumb in sight.

This type of Headteacher announcement always came at the end of meetings so that she could make a quick exit and the victim then receive the compassion, sympathy and, 'rather you than me', looks from the rest of the staff. Beryl also left the room quite quickly, no doubt seeking more comfort food. Poor Mrs Bunter didn't walk or run anywhere, she rolled. But not a forward or backward roll like in a P.E. lesson, her speciality was more like a cheese roll smothered with sweet pickle. When she walked into the staffroom the teachers either hid their food or finished it off quickly. Her idea of a balanced diet

131

was a measuring scale with a cream cake on one side and two doughnuts on the other.

Was this type of role a punishment from the Head for being overweight, or an incentive for her to lose it? Did Beryl know that some of the older pupils impersonated her behind her back by puffing out their cheeks and walking from side to side in a wider pose with arms away from their body, a bit like a gorilla?

Over the next few months Beryl gave everyone the impression that she was taking her new responsibility very seriously. The staff wondered what went through her mind, apart from eating lots of food, when she was putting up posters about 5 a day, healthier lifestyle, chocolate free packed lunches and regular exercise. Perhaps, after all, this was a cunning plan by Ms Steak: lead a healthy lifestyle or you too will grow up to look like Beryl Bunter. That would work for me. BB seemed to carry on being her old sweet self, the staff automatically hid their food when she walked into the staffroom, or if there wasn't much left they crammed as much as possible into their mouths in a hamster impersonation.

About six months later, Mrs Bunter announced her own surprise news to Jos Steak, and the rest of the staff, she was expecting a baby, her first, and she was due in six weeks. She would be starting her maternity leave in three weeks' time, but unlikely to return to her class after that.

Beryl Bunter

There were several reasons why this came as such a shock to the teachers. Firstly, no one actually noticed that she was putting on any additional weight. Her natural camouflage had hidden this fact well. Secondly, female eating habits and normal moods can change, but again no clues were given out. Finally, a teacher would normally confide her secret with someone on the staff but no, not BB. Perhaps the healthy living coordinator post had finally made up her mind that now was the moment for a family of her own. Ms Steak was obviously rather surprised by this announcement and the absolute miniMum amount of notice that could be given to the school about the expected week of birth. Maternity leave posts were notoriously one of the most difficult jobs to cover due to their temporary nature and erratic length of time working. The teacher going on the maternity break held most of the top cards in this game of bluff and suspense. Any maternity post cannot be offered as a new permanent, full-time vacancy until the teacher resigned in writing. This could be up to around a year after the baby was born and a worrying time in limbo for schools and parents.

The third member of staff to have quickly entered the character category was none other than Ms Jos Steak. Despite only coming to the end of her first year here, she had made enormous strides to break into this unique and select group. It had not been an easy start for her, Mr Bush (bless him), had left a lot of things incomplete and even more not started at all. Maybe the stress was getting to her, if not that then something else was definitely niggling at her.

I first noticed it at the Easter drama production that took place one evening after school in the hall. I helped a few others to set up all the chairs for the audience. We brought seats from various classrooms and arranged five rows of twenty chairs. However, when we returned two hours later for the play they had all been rearranged. They were still in five rows of twenty but all the chairs that were the same pattern or style as each other were all on the same row or half row. The caretaker told us that Ms Steak had given a shriek when she walked into the hall an hour ago and spent all that time swapping them about. If they had coloured, plastic moulds on the end of the feet then all the same colours were now together! Why? What did it matter, they were all chairs!

The following morning during break time we were in the staffroom topping up on caffeine when Jos came in and started washing up anything that was in the sink. She even washed the cups up that were on the draining board and they were clean. After completing that, she looked around for more. Gradually, she removed the mugs and cups from the teachers and assistants who were sitting nearest to the sink and washed them up. This baffled and annoyed many of them as they were only half way down the drink and felt they would not have enough inside to help them make it through to the lunch break. Sensing the growing annoyance in the room she retreated to the sanctuary of her office but on the way out she opened and closed the door three times before passing through it. "She's cracked early," offered Mr Hart, "I knew she was weak, they should have appointed a man."

On that note, he felt it was probably a good idea to flee the staffroom before the female retaliation rained down on him. Over the next few weeks, I noticed that every time I passed near to the Head's office she was cleaning, sorting or tidying. Sometimes it looked like the same files and drawers that she had done earlier in the week.

One day, Ms Steak was heading down to the playground and I was about three metres behind her. I thought she had slipped or stumbled as she changed her step pattern mid-stride. I then realised that she was carefully making sure that she didn't tread on any of the joins or cracks on the path, always placing each step in the middle. This must be, 'Headteacher Hopscotch', a senior management strategy to relieve stress I thought.

A few weeks later, I overheard two of my colleagues talking about OCD, I had no idea what it was, they were three letters I had never heard put together. When I returned to my classroom, I tapped them into the search engine on my computer and read the words, 'Obsessive Compulsive Disorder'. After reading the explanation it meant only one thing – our Headteacher. Usually linked to stress, the symptoms described all the odd things that Jos had been doing over the past few months and also listed some that we were yet to experience.

Out of the corner of my eye I noticed that there were several teachers next door talking to our Deputy Head, Mrs Form. They were all the senior members of staff and it didn't take a genius to work out who and what they were talking about. A few days later our local authority inspector, Miss Claws, turned up for an unexpected visit, spent an hour talking to Jos and the next thing we heard was that our Head was,

Ms Steak OCD

'working from home', and Mrs Form had taken over as our leader temporarily.

Why would anyone in their right mind want to be a Headteacher, with people moaning to you, or about you, all day? You came into the job to teach and the more successful you were the less you actually taught, until they finally take your class away and you sit in an office shuffling papers, drinking tea, filling out forms and going to endless meetings. I would never want to be a Head. I think you must either be mad to become one or you go mad shortly after you've been appointed.

CHAPTER EIGHTEEN

SPORTS' DAY - CAN'T WAIT!

The annual Sports' Day can mean many things to different people of various ages. Obviously some children thrive in a competitive, sporting environment and it is one of the days in the school year that they look forward to the most. It is their icing on the cake day, a day to shine out strongly as, 'simply the best'. Usually, there will be one or two children of each gender in each year group who slot into this category. Depending on their overall ability it will either be their annual opportunity to win everything, or to win the most at their own school sports because at the next level up of inter school competition they will probably not be in the first three.

Other children can avoid the day with a passion, if possible they will be ill, injured or enter no events and hope no one noticed their absence. Teachers will sometimes create races for similar children to race against each other and everyone knows why. Of course, the vast majority of children are somewhere in between these extremes knowing that they are often the support act but hoping to do well and enjoy the day.

Quite often the most nervous, agitated and unreasonable ones on such days are the so called grown-ups, the mothers and fathers who lived their lives through their own child. Parents often lost sleep thinking about their child before the so called, 'big day'. Some would try to be proactive in the build-up to the races by discussing strategy and tactics leading up to Sports day. Though this could be a little too obvious when six year old Oscar was the only one in the race to take up the classic sprinter position of professional athletes as seen on television. Running spikes worn by a seven year old can also be seen as taking things just a tad too far but believe you me it did happen.

No child wanted to let their parents down and no parents wanted to be embarrassed by their offspring. However, the 'winning at all costs' type of parent can be an utter humiliation to all concerned. Parents and guardians have been known to deliberately position themselves on or very near the finish line and even produced film evidence almost as quickly as a television replay to prove that their child was really placed higher than the position they were given.

Sometimes there can be rivalry from families who lived in the same street or worked together or were related in some way. For many parents, it was simply enough if their child was not last, didn't fall, or get injured and ended the race happy. Oh, for more and more of those families.

Cheats do still exist though, ranging from the Egg and Spoon with added chewing gum, blu-tak or a sticky thumb on top to secure the shaky object on board. Beware of the child who brought his/her own equipment to use e.g. sack, skipping rope, spoon or ball. Even the pre-school child's race can be

Oscar Sprint Position

spoilt by the over enthusiastic parent willing to pick up their child and run them to the finish line or dragged them behind nearly pulling an arm from its socket. Actual parent races have rapidly declined over the years due to many of the previously mentioned reasons. Is it any wonder that many schools have searched for the win for all and no one loses solution? But life is not like that and I doubt if we do our children any favours by fixing such sports events. Perhaps a happy medium could be found somehow?

Have you noticed that certain popular races, from when the previous generation attended primary schools, have disappeared from the sport's day programme? These include both the traditional style and the modern combination of the three legged, sack, slow bicycle, obstacle, dressing up, piggy back races and the tug of war. So called Health and Safety regulations have a lot to answer for in England.

Our school chess team had been practising hard all year. Once again we had won the County Championship and went on to represent it in the National Tournament. I felt that we had a good chess team this year, but then what did I know? Children's chess knowledge can vary over the term and sometimes it was hard to choose the correct board order. In these tournaments, we had to name six players and they were placed in strength order according to their chess ability. Board one had to be the best player in the team and board six the playing reserve. Our six were very different players. Although this was a team competition, it was hard to escape from the fact that chess was very much an individual sport. This year's national finals took place over a weekend in London, our Under 11 team was:

Board One – Sean the Autistic. He will never look at his opponent but is a brilliant strategist with an amazing memory for combinations and patterns of games from the past.

Board Two – Blind Barry. He uses a special Braille chess board to run his fingers over to remind himself where all the pieces are positioned. Barry even knows if someone moves a piece when they shouldn't and where it has come from.

Board Three – Carole the Tomboy. She prefers to be known as Simon and realised from an early age that more boys than girls play chess so thought it must be for her/him.

Board Four – Mohammed Khan. He can outstare anyone without having to blink (apart from Barry). An amazing memory for recalling every game he has ever played and all the moves.

Board Five – Vladi Noosenz. The new kid on the block and despite only being a Year 4 pupil he is in the team on merit. Wonderful and so appropriate to have a 'Czech' chess player.

Board Six – Plain Jane Crane. Boys simply cannot take their eyes off her. So distracting with her long, blonde hair and heavenly smile that she won most of her games without actually being that strong a player. Boys fail to concentrate in her presence and make silly moves or forget to press their clock and lose on time. Most of her losses are when playing against other girls.

Our weekend away went really well. After completing our six matches we had won four and lost two. The two defeats were against schools from the independent sector that had once again proved too strong for us. However, we did finish in the top 10 state schools for the country, a fantastic achievement. I was really proud of our team as well as being proud of myself for helping them so much during the year.

CHAPTER NINETEEN

'ARE YOU SITTING COMFORTABLY? THEN I'LL BEGIN'

Have you ever read one of those soppy stories where the young girl met her Prince Charming, accidentally, but they discovered that they really loved each other. Later, they married in a castle and lived happily ever. Yuk! I always hated those stories as a little girl, what a load of drivel, rubbish, that just doesn't happen in the real world...does it?

The following morning I remembered that it was the weekend of the Championship play-offs and Cliff had left me four tickets for the Wembley occasion on the bank holiday Monday at the end of May. The team had to meet up for a final training session on the Saturday before travelling down to London and staying over in a hotel in preparation for the final.

I always slept a lot at the weekends. It's amazing how exhausted you can feel after a full week of teaching. On the Saturday afternoon, Alfie and I met up with a few of my friends from the ladies football team. Shopping did not impress my canine friend apart from when we visited 'Dogs R Us'. Three of my team mates said that they would like to go to the play-off final where Cliff's team was playing Chelnal Coldpoint County from London.

On the Monday we travelled down in Vicki's car, so we made good time, and parked up about half a mile from the ground and walked the rest. There were thousands of people milling about from both teams but all well behaved, thank goodness. The seats were excellent, close to the half way line and it was great that Cliff actually spotted us and waved before the game started. The first half was quite dull really with both teams cancelling each other out and 0-0 was a true reflection of the game. During the second half the game livened up but Cliff seemed rather subdued, probably due to the two players who always seemed to be on him as soon as the ball came in his direction. But that created space for other players and Mancpool took the lead half way through the second half and held on to it despite enormous pressure from Chelnal.

A fantastic result and Cliff would be back in the Premiership next season – if they renewed his contract. We met up with him a couple of hours after the final whistle. It was obvious that some of the celebratory champagne had sprayed down his throat by the way he spoke and walked. He took us all out for a meal afterwards and completely embarrassed me towards the end of the evening by producing a small box from his pocket, going down on one knee and asking me to marry him! Wow, I thought it was a dream at first but no this was indeed the real world. I cried, then said, "Yes!", and cried some more. I rang my Mum shortly after and guess what? Yes, she cried.

Much to my amazement, Cliff had already booked the wedding at a local castle that he knew I adored. It was to be the

Wonderful Wedding

second weekend of the school summer holidays with a two week honeymoon in St Lucia, a place that had always fascinated me since we had studied it in a school comparison project – so the National Curriculum did have some uses.

The remainder of the summer term just flew by and I think I floated on in dreamland for most of it. There were so many things to be sorted out for a wedding, especially when it happened to be yours! The invitations were always a problem and it was a hard decision but I didn't invite anyone from school – apart from Mr Bush, but then he wasn't there anymore. The wedding at Carys Castle was just fantastic. It was a good job that we had it videoed as most of the day was a blurry haze to me. One thing that I will always remember was coming out of the Church and walking, with my husband… through the guard of honour just outside the castle. The first half of the guard was from the two football teams, Mancpool Town players on one side and my team mates from Albion Myway Wanderers on the opposite side. But just after them was my Recorder Club from school holding up their instruments in an upside down 'V' shape for us to stoop under. I was just about over that surprise when I heard the school choir in the shape of my class with their own words about me to the tune of, 'Match of the Day', a tune I now knew very well.

Afterwards, I could only remember snippets of my special day. Bits kept coming back to me over the next few weeks, like the sign at the back of the castle Chapel that read, 'Would the congregation please note that the bowl at the back of the Church labelled FOR THE SICK is for monetary donations only'.

My Dad was very proud to lead me down the aisle to 'give me away'. Both families got on really well, my best friend Helen was the chief bridesmaid with several of my young cousins trailing along behind her. Cliff's best man was his brother Ricky (known as Rocky).

There wasn't much time after we returned from honeymoon before the new school year started. Barry Bubble called round to see me with the news that Jos Steak was returning after a short spell in hospital and a long rest at home. But poor Chlora Form, our Deputy Head, had one collision too many with her garden wall at home and had her neck in a special support brace. The chances were that she would not be returning to school again. That was sad, so who would be the new Deputy Head – Mr Hart I suppose? When I agreed to marry Cliff Link I did say to him quite firmly that I really didn't want to lose my surname. I loved the name Ing. So I agreed to take his name, as was the normal tradition, and add it on, so that in the future my name would be Ms Sarah Ing-Link.

Cliff started back at football before I was due to be in school. You can't really call playing football work though, can you? But he was paid for it and Mancpool had given him a new three year contract but with penalty clauses in it for being booked or sent off.

I went into my classroom four or five times to prepare for the new class and the new school year. It felt really strange to see my new name on the door. How long would it take the children to remember that my name was now Ms Ing-Link?

A TEACHER'S TEN MOST ANNOYING PEOPLE

1.   Child – the know all who interrupts everyone, including the teacher.

2.   Parent – who stops you in the street, smiles sweetly, makes polite conversation and then asks how their child is getting on at school.

3.   Headteacher – the one who goes on a course and immediately starts to change what you are doing in school to fit with the views of the course. Until they go on one with alternative ideas.

4.   Deputy Head – befriends teachers but then tells tales to the Head in an attempt to gain his/her first Headship.

5.   Governor – who thinks they are equal to an inspector and should be bowed to and their child given special treatment at the school.

6.   Inspector (local authority) – pretends to know all about you, smiles sympathetically but does nothing to help, a pretender.

7.   Ofsted Inspector – likes to frighten teachers by their presence, deliberately sits in their eye line during an

observation, writes copious notes that say nothing but makes themself look good.

8.   Caretaker – who thinks he can sing, and proves himself wrong every day.

9.   Secondary school teacher – one who believes, and tells their class, that education starts at Year 7.

10.   Volunteer Parent – ones who are not there to help, just to see how their own child is doing and make friends with the teacher.

This is the second book in the 'Miss Ing' series. The first is called 'Miss Ing – Teacher (NQT)'.

Website address for further information
about the author and illustrator:

www.sidwalesauthor.co.uk